ABENG

MICHELLE CLIFF was born in Jamaica and is the author of three ac-
claimed novels: *Abeng*; its sequel, *No Telephone to Heaven*; and *Free Enterprise*. She has also written two collections of short stories, *Bodies of
Water* and *The Store of a Million Items*, and two poetry collections, *The
Land of Look Behind* and *Claiming an Identity They Taught Me to Despise*.
Her works explore the various, complex identity problems that stem
from a colonized world, as well as the difficulty of establishing an authentic, individual identity despite race and gender constructs.

Praise for *Abeng*

"The beauty and authority of her writing is coupled in a rare way
with profound insight." —Toni Morrison

"Michelle Cliff has a keen eye for detail . . . her pithy anecdotal descriptions bring Jamaica's present and past to life."
—*The New York Times Book Review*

"Jamaican history, lore, and landscapes are evocatively re-created
in this multilayered novel. . . . Through its richness and diversity of
detail, Abeng achieves a timeless universality." —*Publishers Weekly*

"*Abeng* is a solid achievement, a book that offers a wealth of history
and culture. . . . [Cliff's] perception of character, her receptivity to
sensuous detail, her rendering of the language, make our journey . . .
a richly textured experience." —*Plexus*

"Jamaican history and mythology almost become characters in this
multilayered novel, and the knowledge of history, particularly the history of suffering, is presented as the way to understand the present."
—*Ms. Magazine*

Praise for *No Telephone to Heaven*

"Structurally ambitious and innovative, making tangible through its form a vivid, spiraling tension between past and present . . . a triumph of artistic integration, a hard-won harmony between the political and the personal, between realism and the mysteries of the spirit."   —*The Washington Post Book World*

"I am in awe of Michelle Cliff's achievement. The work is lyrical, intelligent, full of a moral passion kept taut and spare and absolutely unsentimental. The range of her knowledge, insight, and compassion is astonishing."   —Janette Turner Hospital

"A tour de force. I very much admire what she does with language, and the fact that she's struggling with central issues of our time. A powerful book, truly a stupendous achievement: the complex sense of Jamaica with its anguish and its beauty. In her generation, Cliff is rare and is already distinguished as a writer of great substance and power."   —Tillie Olsen

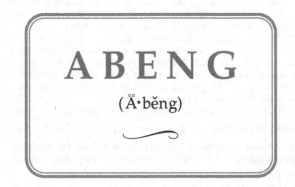

ABENG
(Å·bĕng)

Michelle Cliff

A PLUME BOOK

PLUME
Published by the Penguin Group
Penguin Group (USA) Inc., 375 Hudson Street, New York, New York 10014, U.S.A. •
Penguin Group (Canada), 90 Eglinton Avenue East, Suite 700, Toronto, Ontario, Canada
M4P 2Y3 (a division of Pearson Penguin Canada Inc.) • Penguin Books Ltd., 80 Strand,
London WC2R 0RL, England • Penguin Ireland, 25 St. Stephen's Green, Dublin 2,
Ireland (a division of Penguin Books Ltd.) • Penguin Group (Australia), 250 Camberwell
Road, Camberwell, Victoria 3124, Australia (a division of Pearson Australia Group Pty.
Ltd.) • Penguin Books India Pvt. Ltd., 11 Community Centre, Panchsheel Park, New
Delhi — 110 017, India • Penguin Group (NZ), 67 Apollo Drive, Rosedale, North Shore
0632, New Zealand (a division of Pearson New Zealand Ltd) • Penguin Books (South
Africa) (Pty.) Ltd., 24 Sturdee Avenue, Rosebank, Johannesburg 2196, South Africa

Penguin Books Ltd., Registered Offices: 80 Strand, London WC2R 0RL, England

Published by Plume, a member of Penguin Group (USA) Inc. Previously published in
Obelisk and Penguin editions. Originally published by The Crossing Press.

First Plume Printing, September 1995
20 19 18 17 16 15 14 13 12 11

℗ REGISTERED TRADEMARK—MARCA REGISTRADA

LIBRARY OF CONGRESS CATALOGING-IN-PUBLICATION DATA

Cliff, Michelle.
    Abeng / Michelle Cliff.
        p. cm.
    ISBN 978-0-452-27483-9
    1. Feminism—Fiction. I. Title.
PR9265.9.C55A63   1995
813—dc20   95-14134
                            CIP

Printed in the United States of America
Set in Palatino

PUBLISHER'S NOTE
This is a work of fiction. Names, characters, places, and incidents are either the product
of the author's imagination or are used fictitiously, and any resemblance to actual persons,
living or dead, business establishments, events, or locales is entirely coincidental.

to the memory of Jean Toomer—
and for Bessie Head

> *To know birth and to know death*
> *In one emotion,*
> *To look before and after with one eye. . . .*
> *To know the World and be without a World:*
> *In this light that is no light,*
> *This time that is no time, to be*
> *And to be free. . . .*

Basil McFarlane, b. 1922,
Jamaican poet.

Abeng is an African word meaning conch shell. The blowing of the conch called the slaves to the canefields in the West Indies. The *abeng* had another use: it was the instrument used by the Maroon armies to pass their messages and reach one another.

For some of the details of this book, I am indebted to the work of Zora Neale Hurston, Jervis Anderson, and Orlando Patterson. I also owe a debt to Olive Lewin and the Jamaican Folksingers, for their beautiful and faithful recording of traditional Jamaican music. I am grateful to the MacDowell Colony, where much of this was written. I need to thank those who read the manuscript and gave me support and criticism—Audre Lorde, Irena Klepfisz, Clare Coss, Susan Wood-Thompson, Beth Brant, Denise Dorsz, and Adrienne Rich. I also want to thank Nancy K. Bereano of Crossing Press for her support, enthusiasm, and intelligence during a difficult time.

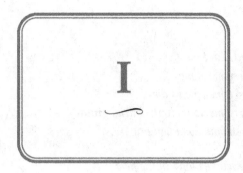

I

Lord, Lord
Carry me alone
Carry me when I die
Carry me down to the burial groun'
Hush you, doan you cry.

I've worked long in the field
I've handled plenty of hoe
To plough the cane
And hoe the groun'
And hear the sugar cane grow.

Lord, Lord
Carry me alone
Carry me when I die
Carry me down to the burial groun'
Hush you, doan you cry.

—slave lament, traditional.

Chapter One

The island rose and sank. Twice. During periods in which history was recorded by indentations on rock and shell.

This is a book about the time which followed on that time. As the island became a place where people lived. Indians. Africans. Europeans.

~

It was a Sunday morning at the height of the height of the mango season. High July—and hot. No rain probably until October—at least no rain of any consequence.

There was a splendid profusion of fruit. The slender cylinders of St. Juliennes hung from a grafted branch of a common mango tree in a backyard in town. Round and pink Bombays seemed to be everywhere—brimming calabashes in the middle of dining tables, pouring out of crates and tumbling onto sidewalks. Small and orange number elevens filled the market baskets at Crossroads, the baskets carried on the heads of women traveling to town from country. Green and spotted Black mangoes dotted the ground at bus stops, school-yards, country stores—these were only to be gathered, not sold. The fruit was all over and each variety was unto itself—with its own taste, its own distinction of shade and highlight, its own occasion and use. In the yards around town and on the hills in the country, spots of yellow, pink, red, orange, black, and green appeared between the almost-blue elongated leaves of the fat and laden trees—and created a confusion underneath.

The Savages—father, mother, and two daughters—were getting ready for church, the first service of the day. "This is the day the Lord has made. Let us rejoice and be glad in it." Mr. Savage chanted as he shaved. The girls were bickering over something or other in the room they shared, and at the same time filling their small plastic purses with a shilling for collection, clean handkerchief with SUNDAY embroidered in the corner, and a ripe number eleven.

It seemed to many people that all the children on the island were carrying pieces of the fruit with them. Khaki pockets bulged out of shape with roundness and in defiance—just one slip on the pavement could release juice or sap, and there would be hell to pay. Mouths everywhere burned from the sap and tingled from the juice; teeth caught the hairs from the seed and tightened around the yellow and gold fibers—even though there was bounty, it was important to reach every last bit of flesh—to complete the mango, and move on to the next.

It was as if the island was host to some ripe sweet plague. Because of the visitation, peppermint and chocolate sales had dropped off, so had paradise plums, bullah cakes—and the Fudgie men who peddled popsicles from wooden boxes on the backs of their bicycles noticed fewer responses to their cry of FUDGEEEE. The new-to-the-island soft custard stand on the Halfway Tree Road reported that they were not doing very well, but expected sales to pick up in the heat of August, when the mangoes would be finished and the avocado would be in season.

Mangotime was not usually such a business, but this was 1958 and the biggest crop in recent memory—as the *Daily Gleaner* itself reported. The paper ran an editorial which spoke of God's Gift to Jamaica, and concluded by telling all inhabitants to be hospitable to the tourists.

Some of the mystery and wonder of mangotime may have been in the fact that this was a wild fruit. Jamaicans did not cultivate it for export to America or England—like citrus, cane, bananas. So much was this so, that when walking through Harlem or Notting Hill Gate, Brooklyn or Ladbroke Grove, island people were genuinely shocked to see a Bombay, half-ripe usually ("Picked much too young"), nesting in a bed of green excelsior, showing through a display window, priced out of reach ("Lord, have mercy, we use them to stone dogs back home"), and they wondered where the mango had come from. Someone somewhere else must be exporting the fruit. For them, the mango was to be kept an island secret.

They did not cultivate the mango, but they made occasional efforts to change the course of its development. These efforts were usually few and far between and carried out with care and discretion. A branch was sliced from a common mango tree and replaced with a branch from a St. Julienne—the former could withstand all manner of disease or weather; the latter was fragile. But the Jamaican taste was growing for the St. Julienne, which was judged to be consistently full and deep in its sweetness, while the common mango was termed unpredictable, with a sweetness that could be thin and might leave an aftertaste. That was as far as cultivation went in 1958, though—a few grafts here and there—they did not tamper further.

There were other wild fruit on the island—the bush of Jamaica had long been written about as one of the most naturally fruitful places on earth—but the mango was supreme among all other growing things—the paragon: "Mother Sugar herself."

It was a surprising fruit—sometimes remaining hidden for years behind vines and underbrush—saving its sweetness for wild pigs and wild birds.

In 1958 Jamaica had two rulers: a white queen and a white governor. Independence-in-practically-name-only was four years away. The portrait of the white queen hung in banks, department stores, grocery stores, schools, government buildings, and homes—from countryside shanties to the split-levels on the hills above Kingston Harbor. A rather plain little white woman decked in medals and other regalia—wearing, of course, a crown. Our-lady-of-the-colonies. The whitest woman in the world. Elizabeth II, great-granddaughter of Victoria, for whom the downtown crafts market—where women came from the countryside to sell their baskets and Rastafarians sold their brooms and old Black men sold their wood-carvings to the passengers of cruise ships and Pan-American Clippers—was named.

The monetary system of the island was based on the pounds/shillings/pence of the "mother" country. The coins and notes were similar to those struck and printed for Great Britain itself. The coins came from the Royal Mint and the notes from the Bank of England, popularly called the Old Lady of Threadneedle Street. There were two basic differences: Jamaican money bore the word JAMAICA, and the sovereign crest of the island—an Arawak Indian and a white conqueror: only one of these existed in 1958.

The population of the island was primarily Black ("overwhelmingly," some sources said), with gradations of shading reaching into the top strata of the society. Africans were mixed with Sephardic Jews, Chinese, Syrians, Lebanese, East Indians—but the large working class, and class of poor people, was Black.

It was the Sunday custom of the Savages to attend their first church service at the John Knox Memorial Church at Constant Spring. Of light brown stucco, the long low building had mahogany louvers running the length of the two far aisles—the louvers were turned down against the sun. The pews were also mahogany, and were divided down the middle by one single center aisle. The church was spare and clean in its design—the only decoration, if that is what it could be called, was a large cross behind the pulpit, carved of Godwood—the original tree—the tree of Eden. Commonly known as the birch gum.

There was no church choir at John Knox; a Scottish schoolteacher played Presbyterian hymns at a harpsichord, which had been shipped to Jamaica in a box and was reassembled by the minister. The instrument had never adjusted to the climate. The schoolteacher explained to the congregation that a harpsichord had to be tuned each time it was to be played; even so, tuning upon tuning never made the instrument sound quite right. There was a gravelly tinkle in its voice, far more than a harpsichord is supposed to have, and it was easily drowned out by the passing traffic, the voices of the congregation, the pair of croaking lizards who lived behind the cross of Godwood, sounding a double bass in the wrong tempo, as the schoolteacher tinkled out the prelude, when the congregation entered, and the postlude, when they left the church. Although they were not able to say so, most of the congregation felt that the harpsichord had been a mistake—not meant even in the most perfect of climatic conditions to accompany a hundred voices. It seemed that English people must sing softer—or not at all—and that the climate of that place—damp and dreary—surpassed the clear light and deep warmth of Jamaica. They had always thought their island climate a gift; the harpsichord told them different. The schoolteacher advised the congregation to tone down their singing, to consider the nuances of harmony and quiet—but this didn't work.

The minister of the church was a red-faced Englishman, who preached plainly and briefly, and had been a major in the King's Household Cavalry during the last war. He had emigrated to Jamaica in 1949, and since then had spent his afternoons at the bar of the South Camp Hotel, where he drank beer and played skittles with English soldiers and merchant seamen. On special days he led the congregation in "God Save the Queen"—during the Suez Crisis of 1956 they had stood and sung it every Sunday for a month. On other, more ordinary Sundays, they sang the standards—"Onward Christian Soldiers, Marching as to War"; "Faith of Our Fathers, Living Still, in Spite of Dungeon, Fire and Sword"; "Fairest Lord Jesus, Ruler of All Nature"; "Fling Out the Banner, Let It Float, Skyward and Seaward, High and Wide"—in which the banner of righteousness carried by the Christian soldiers mingled with the Union Jack.

The congregation at John Knox was Black and white—Jamaican and English and American. Mostly of the middle class. The church was Mr. Savage's choice for worship.

In 1958, and for some time before, the two most socially prestigious churches in Kingston were Holy Cross, the cathedral at Halfway Tree, and the Kingston Parish Church, downtown on King Street, near King's Parade, founded in 1692.

Holy Cross Cathedral was the church of the island's wealthy Catholics—most of them Lebanese and Syrian and Chinese, some Spanish. These were the same people who sent their daughters to the Convent of the Immaculate Conception, a group of pink-stucco Spanish-tiled-roof villas, set back on green lawns next to a golf course. The Protestants sent their daughters to St. Catherine's, a red-brick girls' school, which was less grand but more severe than Immaculate Conception.

The Parish Church was High Anglican—it was the church of attendance of the white governor, and members of the royal family stopped there when the queen's yacht, *H. M. S. Britannia*, docked in Kingston Harbor. A very large stone edifice, it was foursquare and had been built to last. A rood screen had been imported from a church in Canterbury; a choir loft had been carved by a team of local craftsmen—in 1820, before the slaves were freed.

In 1958, while digging near the churchyard during some renovations to the building, workers uncovered a coffin of heavy metal—a coffin of huge proportions. Not the shape of a coffin at all—shaped like a monstrous packing case, made of lead and welded shut. A brass plate which had been affixed to the coffin and etched with an inscription informed the vicar that the coffin contained the remains of a hundred plague victims, part of a shipload of slaves from the Gold Coast, who had contracted the plague from the rats on the vessel which brought them to Jamaica. Others, many others, would have died onboard and their bodies dropped in the sea along the Middle Passage—the route across the Atlantic from Africa—or the Windward Passage—the route from the Atlantic to the islands of the Caribbean Sea. The people in the coffin had died in a *barracoon* in Kingston—a holding pen—a stockade.

The coffin should be opened on no account, the plaque said, as the plague might still be viable. The vicar commissioned an American navy warship in port to take the coffin twenty miles out and sink it in the sea.

After the morning service, the Savages left Constant Spring and drove to their house on Dunbarton Crescent, where Dorothy, the Black woman who worked for them, prepared Sunday dinner. When the family had eaten, and she had cleaned up, she caught the bus to Trench Town, where her three-year-old daughter lived with Dorothy's mother. The Savages left also, for their weekly seabath at Tumbleover, a rocky and wild beach, unsheltered by cove or harbor, opposite the mangrove swamps on the Palisadoes Road, between Kingston Airport and the Gypsum factory at Rock Fort—a fort built by the Spanish, with the cannon still in place.

There was a wicked undertow at Tumbleover, and huge waves unbroken by a reef. Underneath the water was smooth rock covered with slippery sealife, and no foothold to be had. Once in the waves, a swimmer had to relax and ride the breakers—far out and then in. The beach was usually deserted, with only the water's force as background noise, and occasional planes circling to land at Palisadoes.

A Sunday afternoon not long before this Sunday afternoon, Clare, the elder Savage daughter, who was twelve years old, found a trilobite fossil embedded in the rocks under the water, and Mr. Savage had explained in great detail how old the world was, and how insignificant was man.

"Clare, if you took a broomstick; or if you took an obelisk from ancient Egypt, like Cleopatra's Needle, and made a pinprick at the tip—that would represent the history of mankind; the rest all came before us. Think about it. Consider it."

Clare's relationship with her father took the form of what she imagined a son would have, if there had been a son. Mr. Savage took his daughter to a mountaintop to prove to her that the island had exploded from the sea. True to his theory—she was his daughter; she assumed the idea belonged to him—there were fragments of seashells and pieces of coral on top. He explained to her how the entire chain of the West Indies had once been underwater. He spoke of mountainfolding, the process by which flat rock becomes peaks and slopes. While this process usually took thousands of years, Mr. Savage preferred to believe that Jamaican mountains had been created in cataclysm. All of a sudden.

Perhaps, he said to his daughter, the islands of the West Indies—particularly the Greater Antilles, which were said once to have been joined—were the remains of Atlantis, the floating continent Plato had written about in the *Timaeus*, that sank under the sea. It had been an ideal place, too good for this world. "But then there was a great and powerful earthquake, and the continent came back up again—and was first joined in a chain and then was split apart into islands." He stopped; then thought further. "Or maybe the islands were an undersea mountain range, and emerged when Atlantis went under the Mediterranean. When the volcano erupted in Crete." He paused again.

"Some say that Crete and Atlantis were one," still trying to forge some connection between the pieces of knowledge he possessed, and how he wanted things to be.

Mr. Savage was fascinated by myth and natural disaster. He collected books on Stonehenge, the Pyramids, the Great Wall of China—he knew the details of each ancient structure and was convinced that all were connected to some magical source—some "divine plan," he said. Nothing, to him, was ever what it seemed to be. Nothing was an achievement of human labor. Devising arch and circle; creating brick from straw and mud and hauling stones to the site of construction. Mr. Savage was a believer in extraterrestrial life—in a mythic piece of machinery found in a bed of coal: part of a spaceship, he concluded; proof that we had been visited by beings from another planet, who might be observing us even now. Most people thought him focused out, most of the time, while they were focused in, or down. "Down to earth," was what they called his wife—sometimes his complement, sometimes his opposite. To pass the time until his deliverance, he

went to the racetrack, courted women on the sly, drank rum and water, and moved from job to job, while his wife kept her faith, saved
her own money from her job in a downtown hotel, spoke sometimes
with her relatives, and prayed for a better day.

Clare's father was no commonplace dreamer, one whose visions
were only slightly distorted by rum; he didn't have dreams anywhere
near the realm of accomplishment. His visions—which included the
second coming, the end of the world, Armageddon—would be
achieved only by waiting; only through intervention from the outside—
when God judged the time was right. In the meanwhile he tried to
pass these ideals on to his elder daughter—calling her an Aztec princess, golden in the sun. "Clare, you would have certainly been a choice
for sacrifice—you know the Aztecs slaughtered their most beautiful
virgins and drank their blood." It did not occur to Clare to question
her father's reading of history—a worldview in which she would
have been chosen for divine slaughter.

Most often, she became his defender. When he talked about his
notions of space and time and magic to her mother's family, they only
laughed at him. Telling him the planets were but dust. Illusions
created by God to speak of his glory. Dust and shadow was the rest
of the universe. Earth was the one concrete reality. And this life, life
on Earth, just a gateway to the life everlasting. Which was the one
true realm of existence. Many of them only waited to pass into that
realm.

This particular afternoon, Mr. Savage had just stepped into the
water, when he came running and screaming out again—"Shark!
Shark!" He was howling and shaking and pale. He claimed a shark
had swum up right beside his thigh and touched him. Mrs. Savage
went into the water to prove it was safe now, and the girls, Clare and
Jennie, who was seven, followed her. But it was no use. "As God is
my judge," Mr. Savage vowed, "I am never going into the sea again—
never."

In later weeks, the family moved from Tumbleover to Cable Hut,
a beach sheltered by reef and cove, but Mr. Savage only disappeared
into the shed where they sold rum, and reappeared when one of the
girls was sent to get him, and they were ready to leave for home.

Chapter Two

The afternoon of the shark scare the Savages returned home and changed again into church clothes, for the evening service at the Tabernacle of the Almighty on Mountainview Road. Mrs. Savage's place of worship.

The Tabernacle was a small cement-block building separated from the road by a gravel parking lot. Most of the congregation came on foot—the parking lot belonged to the grocery store next door, and the land for the Tabernacle was leased from the shopkeeper, Mr. Chin. The church had aluminum louvers, open to the sounds of cars and the lights of the street, but the building had been baking all day under a zinc roof, and the louvers also let in a breeze from the harbor. At the back of the church the dark outlines of the foothills of the Blue Mountains were shadowed.

As the car drove toward the Tabernacle, Clare could see the congregation moving along the road. All the women seemed to wear the same white plastic-straw hat, and white shoes; their dresses were pastel shades—lime-green, pale blue, light pink. The men were dressed in dark suits, some with a fine gray stripe, light wool or gabardine, and dark shoes and socks. The boy children wore the khaki most Jamaican boys wore, with their school insignia showing in the colors of the epaulets on their shoulders. The girl children were small replicas of the women. Everyone on the road carried a Bible or hymnal in their hands.

The service at the Tabernacle began with Sister Icilda and Sister Girlie singing a duet to the Lord Jesus with their hands folded in on each other in front of their bosoms. Their bottom lips trembled as they strained for the high notes. Secretly—never to their faces—the congregation called them Miss Titty and Miss Tatty, so prim and alike were they. All dressed in white—virginal and deadly serious—they needed no vicar to temper their relationship with the Almighty. This apparent purity seemed to invite ridicule—of which the sisters were entirely oblivious.

After their duet, Brother Emmanuel began as he usually began. Each week pointing a sharply nailed and polished finger at a random communicant (man, woman, or child), and booming: "You . . . You . . .

Brother or Sister . . . are on a slip-pery sli-ide to HELL!" It was the
brother's standard preface to a sermon in which all in the room were
condemned—"unto your children and your children's children"—for
the sin and wretched hopelessness of their lives.

When Brother Emmanuel rested, sitting back in his overstuffed
chair and taking a breath, Sister Shirley pumped the old pump organ
and the congregation rose to her call, led by the choir, to sing hymns
like "Blessed Assurance! Jesus is mine/Oh what a foretaste of glory
divine!/Heir of salvation, purchase of God/Born of His spirit, washed
in His blood." or "Rock of ages, cleft for me/Let me hide myself in
Thee/Let the water and the blood, from Thy wounded side which
flowed/Be of sin the double cure, cleanse me from its guilt and
power."

The hymns at John Knox seemed to suggest a historical and almost equal relationship with the idea of God—that this God would
support the travel of the Word to faraway "climes" and distant "hea-
then" by almost any means necessary—"marching as to war." The
hymns sung by the people in the Tabernacle suggested something
else. The necessity of deliverance. A belief in their eventual redemption. In the balm of Gilead.

During the service—every Sunday evening—someone would be
seized with the spirit, and jump up and fall down moaning, or sway
faster and faster back and forth, calling on God to hear her, asking his
forgiveness. Those so possessed were almost always women. When a
sister got the spirit, two white-gowned sisters came forward to make
sure that the jumping or swaying or fainting communicant would not
do damage to herself. At the start of a full-fledged seizure, Brother
Emmanuel would signal Sisters Icilda and Girlie to start a hymn—
and again all would rise, and Sister Shirley would pump, and the
church would rock back and forth with the vibration of voices, organ,
and possession.

There were more women than men in the church tonight, Clare
thought. There were always more women than men. And the women
became possessed. And the woman sang louder. At times, it occurred
to her, the church seemed only women—as Brother Emmanuel's body,
and his authority, melted into the purple satin of his chair.

The congregation of John Knox was for the most part families—
brown and Black and red and white mothers and fathers and children.
The Tabernacle consisted for the most part of Black women—sitting
and singing in groups and pairs and alone.

When Clare visited her grandmother—her mother's mother—in St. Elizabeth, a parish in the deep country—she sometimes helped her prepare the house for Sunday meeting. The two began on Saturday—cleaning the floors, then waxing them, using half a coconut husk for a brush to bring out the shine on the broad mahogany planks. They dusted and waxed the furniture, and dry-mopped and wet-mopped the painted concrete floor of the porch. On Sunday morning they began by cutting flowers—blossoms of mimosa or mountain pride, blooms of hibiscus or bougainvillea—and putting them into the cut-glass pitcher which Clare's great-grandmother had taken with her when she left her family to run off with one of their servants. This woman, Judith, never saw the family of her mother and father again, but she made her own. She raised five children in a two-room house in the country, with her husband, Mas Samuel, keeping chickens and planting and tending a slope of coffee to keep them going. "Granny," she was called, and Clare had never known her; she had only heard that Granny had become a "bitter old woman," while Mas Samuel became beloved by all around. He outlived his wife by fifteen years, and Clare had known him when she was a baby, but couldn't recollect his face. "Such a sweet brown man. So sweet." That was what people said.

The cut-glass pitcher, carved on its sides with diamond shapes, was all that now remained from Granny's first life. It was prismatic, and split the light in the parlor, casting stripes of color which reflected on the polished floor.

From Judith's second life, there remained the spine of Clare's grandmother's house, two rooms to which two more had been added, one on either side. And Granny's grave, a concrete rectangle at the side of the house next to the flower garden. There was an open book at Granny's head, inscribed with her name and the dates of her life, the names of her dead and living children, and the name of her husband, whose own grave was a yard away.

The pitcher filled with flowers and rainbow sat in the center of the long-legged parlor table on a lace cloth, the family Bible beside it. The old wooden louvers around the room were opened wide to let in the sunlight, because Clare's grandmother, Miss Mattie, did not want to use the kerosene lamps. In the light, spots of dust floated around the room, and Clare, who had been taught about ashes to ashes, dust to dust, liked to think they were bits of the mysterious Granny, whose life and death fascinated her. What she knew of them.

Once the parlor was ready, they went into the yard. Miss Mattie carried her penknife and Clare gathered short sticks, which her grandmother sharpened with the knife—these they put by the front steps, for the members to scrape the red mud from their shoe soles before entering the house. The red mud was clay, heavy and difficult to get off once it dried.

Finally the two—the sorceress and her apprentice, but she wasn't a sorceress, just a woman who led Sunday services—went into the dining room to prepare the communion tray. Slices of a fresh loaf of hard-dough bread were cut into small squares (this is my body, which is broken for you), and Miss Mattie opened her ceremonial bottle of red South African wine and poured some into small glasses which were put on the tray next to the bread (this is my blood, which is shed for you). Clare's grandmother sang softly as she made this ritual, and would not allow her granddaughter to speak or to join in. She closed her eyes briefly over the tray, and then carried it into the parlor, where she placed it on the lower shelf of the long-legged table (this do in remembrance of me). And it caught one of Granny's rainbows. The blood-wine making a mirror in which Clare could detect her own reflection.

Clare was no longer needed. Her grandmother closed all the doors to the parlor and went into her room to dress for the service, and to see that her husband was also dressed. Clare went to the river to meet her friend Zoe, and to swim—she would return only when she knew her grandmother's church was over and the congregation had left.

⁓

In 1733, Nanny, the sorceress, the *obeah*-woman, was killed by a *quashee*—a slave faithful to the white planters—at the height of the War of the Maroons.

Nanny, who could catch a bullet between her buttocks and render the bullet harmless, was from the empire of the Ashanti, and carried the secrets of her magic into slavery. She prepared amulets and oaths for her armies. Her Nanny Town, hidden in the crevices of the Blue Mountains, was the headquarters of the Windward Maroons—who held out against the forces of the white men longer than any rebel troops. They waged war from 1655–1740. Nanny was the magician of

this revolution—she used her skill to unite her people and to conse-
crate their battles.

There is absolutely no doubt that she actually existed. And the
ruins of her Nanny Town remain difficult to reach.

The Tabernacle was alive with voices and movement.

"Um-hmm."

"Oh, yes, Lord. Oh, yes."

"Amen, Brother."

These words were being spoken in ones or twos—together or
distinct—as Brother Emmanuel got into the substance of his sermon.
It was the usual message he gave his congregation every week.
Brother Emmanuel was not a man of any rare gifts of imagination—
he just plied his trade as a man of God, Sunday after Sunday, striving
to be a respected somebody on his own account, as well as trying to
save the souls of his flock from damnation. He was not inspired in his
delivery of the word—for instance, no one could remember him telling a joke to illustrate one of his sermons. Perhaps preachers were not
meant to tell jokes. He had said something funny once, but the joke
was not meant to be. Brother Emmanuel had begun a sentence with
"brethren," then glanced across the congregation and his eyes met
with those of Sisters Icilda and Girlie. His mind reckoned with the
presence of so many women in his congregation, and he matched brethren with "sistern"—which the congregation of course heard as "cis-
tern." Some smiled—Brother Emmanuel coughed, then continued.

Now, he was in full swing—

"No dancing, children . . . No dancing, no movies . . . No dancing,
children, no movies, and no liquor. These t'ings are the work of the
devil. These t'ings serve us not, except to weaken us—in spirit *and* in
body."

"Yes, Brother. Yes. Lord."

"We mus' not smoke the weed, mus' not smoke tobacco, nor
ganja, my children. For with these t'ings, we become as lotos eaters,
and we accomplish no-t'ing in our days."

"Mm-hmm. Yes, Brother. Wunna speak true."

"And let there be no carousing among my flock, no contention between mother and child, husband and wife, sister and brother, woman and man. Contention will mek us weak. Contention will tun us

'gainst one another. Contention will tun us from the Lord Almighty, the maker of heaven and of earth, in whom all t'ings are possible."

"Yes, Brother. Yes, Lord."

"We mus' bide our time. We mus' be patient. We will wait on the Lord. This is the way, children. This is the way to the life everlasting. In which we will all meet over yonder. In the sweet by-and-by. When the trumpet of the Lord shall sound, and the world shall be no more. When the saints of earth have gathered over on the other shore, and the roll is called up yonder I'll be there. When the roll, when the roll is called up yonder, I'll be there."

With that, Sister Shirley pumped the organ and the congregation rose.

In front of the Tabernacle, next to the grocery store which carried dried saltfish and soft drinks and cooking oil and rice and sundries, was a rum shop, where men with crisscrossed red eyeballs swung in and out all hours of the day and all days of the year. Down the road was a moviehouse, the Rialto, which showed triple features of American gangster movies and B-grade westerns and jungle serials starring Johnny Sheffield. There was a shop next to the moviehouse which sold raffle tickets. And another close by which was an offtrack betting parlor, selling wagers on the Epsom Derby and the Grand National at Aintree, as well as the races at home. Number one South Windward Road was known to be a badhouse, where women, gambling, rum, ganja, and all manner of *sint'ing* could be had.

The men who were in the Tabernacle were being sorely tempted. As were their brothers outside. And there was little that Brother Emmanuel could do to alleviate the temptation. To relieve them. The space the temptation entered could not be filled by hymn-singing or sermons, no matter how terrifying. The space had been carved so long ago, carried so long within, it was a historic fact. "Every dog have him day, every puss their four o'clock," was something people said— but saying this was not enough.

The white Jesus, with his chestnut hair, brown eyes, and soft mustache, was handsomer than the white queen, and seemed kinder, but the danger to these men was beyond him. The men—when they worked—were servants to light-skinned or white families; waiters at South Camp, Myrtle Bank, or Courtleigh Manor; porters at Palisadoes Airport. They pumped gas at Texaco or Esso stations. They swept sidewalks. They carried garbage. They cut grass and trimmed hedges. Killed rats. Fed dogs. They balanced trays of Red Stripe beer or Appleton Estate rum on their upturned palms. They were paid with a small brown envelope of cash. They lived from week to week.

The women in the Tabernacle had their spaces of need also—but for most of them, the space had been reduced over time, so that the filling of it became a matter for family. Their anguish in this life became for them identifiable in the faces of the people they were part of. Their pain was unto themselves. As the men's relief was unto themselves. But to the women fell the responsibility for kin—sisters, mothers, children.

The women also served. Cleaned. Mopped. Cooked. Cared for babies lighter than their own. Did other people's laundry. Bought other people's goods in the markets at Crossroads and Constant Spring. They too received some cash each week. To their mothers and sisters and their aunts they gave some toward the care of their children. They saw these children perhaps once a week, if the children were kept in town. Less often if they were not. Many of these women had never been married, but they kept their children and gave them names and supervised their rearing as best they could. Some had been married, but their husbands had left them for America to pick fruit. Or for the north of England to work in factories. Others had husbands employed in households or hotels in different parts of Kingston—these men lived-in, as did their wives—and over the years these people lost touch. So much was ranged against the upkeep of these connections. At times they felt the cause of their losses lay in themselves—their people's *wuthlessness*.

"Like one of the family" was a reality they lived with—taking Christmas with their employers and saving Boxing Day for their own. "Like one of the family" meant staying in a small room with one light and a table and a bed—listening to a sound system which piped in Radio Jamaica. They waited for tea-time and prepared lap trays dressed with starched and ironed linen cloths. They asked missis for the key to the larder so they could remove caddies of Earl Grey or Lapsang Souchong leaves, tins of sardines, English biscuits, Cross and Blackwell or Tipree preserves—gooseberry or greengage plum.

Sometimes this other family became more familiar to them than the people they were closest to. The people they were part of.

An hour a week with Jesus and Brother Emmanuel, backed up by Sisters Icilda and Girlie and the choir, Sister Shirley and her pump organ, eased them somewhat. It was a steady easing—they too lived from week to week. They could count on the ease and there was no one who could take it away from them. They were "washed in the blood of the Lamb."

~~

In the beginning there had been two sisters—Nanny and Sekesu. Nanny fled slavery. Sekesu remained a slave. Some said this was the difference between the sisters.

It was believed that all island children were descended from one or the other. All island people were first cousins.

Chapter Three

*Do-fe-do mek guinea nigger come a Jamaica.**
—proverb

The people in the Tabernacle could trace their bloodlines back to a past of slavery. But this was not something they talked about much, or knew much about. In school they were told that their ancestors had been pagan. That there had been slaves in Africa, where Black people had put each other in chains. They were given the impression that the whites who brought them here from the Gold Coast and the Slave Coast were only copying a West African custom. As though the whites had not named the Slave Coast themselves.

The congregation did not know that African slaves in Africa had been primarily household servants. They were not seasoned. They were not worked in canefields. The system of labor was not industrialized. There was in fact no comparison between the two states of servitude: that practiced by the tribal societies of West Africa and that organized by the Royal African Company of London, chartered by the Crown. These people did not know that one of the reasons the English Parliament and the Crown finally put an end to the slave trade was that because of the Victorian mania for cleanliness, manufacturers needed West African palm oil to make soap—soon the trade

*Translation: Fighting among themselves brought West African slaves to Jamaica.

in palm oil became more profitable than the trade in men and women
and the merchants shifted their investments.

No one had told the people in the Tabernacle that of all the slave
societies in the New World, Jamaica was considered among the most
brutal. They did not know that the death rate of Africans in Jamaica
under slavery exceeded the rate of birth, and that the growth of the
slave population from 1,500 in 1655 to 311,070 in 1834, the year of
freedom, was due *only* to the importation of more people, more
slaves. They did not know that some slaves worked with their faces
locked in masks of tin, so they would not eat the sugar cane as they
cut. Or that there were few white women on the island during slavery, and so the grandmothers of these people sitting in a church on a
Sunday evening during mango season, had been violated again and
again by the very men who whipped them. The rape of Black women
would have existed with or without the presence of white women, of
course, but in Jamaica there was not pretense of civility—all was in
the open.

⌐⌐

Now her head is tied. Now braided. Strung with beads and cowrie
shells. Now she is disguised as a *chasseur*. Now wrapped in a cloth
shot through with gold. Now she stalks the Red Coats as they march
toward her cave, where she spins her Akan chants into spells which
stun her enemies. Calls on the goddesses of the Ashanti forests. Remembers the battle formations of the Dahomey Amazons. She turns
her attention to the hunt. To the cultivation of cassava and yam and
plantain—hiding the places for use in case of flight.

The forests of the island are wild and remind her of Africa. In places
the mountains are no more than cliff-faces. The precipices of these
mountains often hold caves she can use for headquarters or to con-
ceal the weapons of her army. She mixes dyes from roots and teaches
others to cast images on the walls. She collects bark from the trunk
and limbs of the birch gum to touch to the skin of her enemies while
they sweat—and instructs her followers in the natural ways of death.
She moves on her elbows and knees across narrow rock ledges.
Through corridors created by stone.

The entryways are covered in some places with vines—in others
with cascades of water. She teaches her troops to be sure-footed and
to guard the points of access. They hunt with bow and arrow. Spears.
Warclubs. They fill the muskets stolen from plantations with pebbles,

buttons, coins. She teaches them to become bulletproof. To catch a bullet in their left hand and fire it back at their attackers. Only she can catch a bullet between her buttocks—that is a secret she keeps for herself.

She teaches them if they are caught to commit suicide by eating dirt.

—⁓

The capture of the island from the Spanish had been an afterthought. The British fleet, under the command of Penn and Venables, following the orders of the Lord Protector Oliver Cromwell, was unable to take Santo Domingo, and so moved on Jamaica. This took place in 1655. Over the course of the next 180 years, until freedom was obtained in 1834, there was armed, sustained guerrilla warfare against the forces of enslavement. A complex intelligence system between the rebels and the plantation slaves. A network of towns and farms and camps independent from the white planters. An army of thousands—literally thousands—called the Maroons. And this army had moved over the mountains now shadowed at the back of the Tabernacle.

Their name came from *cimarrón*: unruly, runaway. A word first given to cattle which had taken to the hills. Beyond its exact meaning, the word connoted fierce, wild, unbroken.

—⁓

Through the open louvers came the light from the rumshop and the voices of drinkers staggering home. The smell of the sea and the smell of mangoes mixed with each other.

The people in the Tabernacle did not know that their ancestors had been paid to inform on one another: given their freedom for becoming the *blackshots* of the white man. The *blackshot* troops were the most skilled at searching out and destroying the rebels—but they also had a high desertion rate and had been known to turn against their white commanders in battle.

The people in the Tabernacle did not know that Kishee, one of Nanny's commanders, had been killed by Scipio, a Black slave—but of course they did not know who Kishee had been.

They did not know about the Kingdom of the Ashanti or the Kingdom of Dahomey, where most of their ancestors had come from. They did not imagine that Black Africans had commanded thousands of warriors. Built universities. Created systems of law. Devised language. Wrote history. Poetry. Were traders. Artists. Diplomats.

They did not know that their name for papaya—*pawpaw*—was the name of one of the languages of Dahomey. Or that the *cotta*, the circle of cloth women wound tightly to make a cushion to balance baskets on their heads, was an African device, an African word. That Brer Anancy, the spider who inspired tricks and tales, was a West African invention. Or that Cuffee was the name of a Maroon commander— the word had come down to them as *cuffy*, and meant upstart, social climber.

Some of them were called Nanny, because they cared for the children of other women, but they did not know who Nanny had been.

When the English troops advanced on Nanny Town the second time, she decided to move her army across the Blue Mountains—so when the Red Coats arrived the village would be abandoned and the enemy would be confused. At night she and her army set out to find Cudjoe, the leader of the Maroons across the island, and to join with him in a final attack to defeat the whites and take control of the island for the Africans. Her warriors marched in front and behind. In the center of the single file were the women and children, the old people, the young men and women who carried provisions. They had planted all along the route, and Nanny had marked the places where they could take shelter for a day and a night, while the warriors hunted for wild pig, and the others built fires to roast the meat. They marched in this way for over a hundred miles, and finally reached Accompong Town, where Cudjoe and his men were.

A settlement in the Cockpit Country, the land of endless funnels in the earth, the land of look behind. At the heart of the limestone plateau which forms the center of the island. A place of seemingly purposeless crevasses—created when the island sank during the Pliocene Period and the limestone layers dissolved in places—the dissolution stopping where the limestone met with insoluble rock. Swallow-holes. Cockpits. Places to hide. Difficult to reach. Not barren but deep and magnificent indentations populated by bush and growth and wild orchids—collectors of water—natural goblets.

Nanny moved forward to the small dark man with the hump on his back. Cudjoe wore knee-length breeches, an old ragged coat, and a hat with no brim. On his right side he carried a cow's horn of gunpowder and a bag of shots for his musket. From his left shoulder a sheathed cutlass dangled from a strap. His Black skin was reddened from the bauxite in the earth. His followers—those who now surrounded him—were also reddened men. His eyes met with those of Nanny—the small and old Black woman whose only decoration was a necklace fashioned from the teeth of white men. She did not speak, but instructed Kishee to begin the negotiations with Cudjoe. Kishee told him of their plan to join with Cudjoe and his men—the Leeward Maroons—against the Red Coats. He told Cudjoe about the band of Miskito Indians brought to the island to fight against them. The Miskitos—almost every one—had come over to the Maroon side. Through the Miskitos the Windward Maroons had contacted the Spanish on Cuba; and the Spanish governor agreed to respect the freedom of all the Africans on the island, if the rebels won the colony back for Spain.

Cudjoe refused this offer of alliance. He only gave the Windwards temporary refuge before their journey home. They stayed a short time in his camp, then walked back across the plateau and the mountains, through the rainforests, to their own territory.

Not long after, Nanny was murdered, and Cudjoe signed a separate peace with the British governor, in which he was permitted freedom and promised to hunt down other rebels for the Crown. He and his followers became known as the King's Negroes.

Some said he had tired of fighting. Others that he wanted to consolidate his power.

⌐◦

The service was over and the congregation was wishing a "good evening" to Brother Emmanuel. The Savages left with the others and drove home through the by-now-cool night, in which the scent of ripe mangoes was present and heavy. As Mr. Savage drove along the Halfway Tree Road his headlights flashed on the side of Holy Cross— CASTRO SÍ, BATISTA NO. In black paint. In large letters against the cathedral.

Chapter Four

Mr. Savage was caught somewhere between the future and the past—both equal in the imagination. His first name was James, and his middle name, Arthur; in the family and among the friends he kept from school he was called "Boy," sometimes "Boy-Boy," a common enough nickname among a certain class of Jamaicans, an imitation of England, like so many aspects of their lives. Boy came from a family which was known all over Jamaica for its former wealth. His great-grandfather had been sent to the island by the Crown in 1829, to be a puisne (pronounced puny) justice in the parish of St. Ann on the North Coast. This ancestor had originally come from England, and was the son of an earl, but was in Ireland when he was summoned to Jamaica—there acting as a go-between for the king, meeting with Daniel O'Connell, among others, in an effort to stay the movement for Catholic emancipation. He was not successful, and the Catholic Emancipation Act was passed by Parliament the year he left for Jamaica.

The justice was the youngest son in a system governed by primogeniture, and so was forced to set out on his own. Once established in Jamaica he built his first and largest plantation in a place called Runaway Bay—marking his property at the beginning of the drive by twelve Wych elms he brought from his family's estate in Sussex.

As was the custom of many landowners in Jamaica during slavery, the justice did not bring his wife to the island with him. He journeyed by ship to see her three times a year and to renew his business contacts in London, at the Royal African Company and the Tate and Lyle Sugar concern, leaving his overseers in charge of the slaves and the cane. He and his wife were married for ten years, and then she died in childbirth with a measly little daughter who grew up to be an old maid. The justice left his daughter in Sussex with relations and took his son to the plantations on the island.

⌒

By 1958 the original property at Runaway Bay had been subdivided for American vacation homes, and the elm trees were long gone, dying about a hundred years previously—like the harpsichord, the trees never managed to make the adjustment to the Jamaican climate. Clare saw the property for the first time that year, as she drove to the North Coast with her father, who had taken a job as a traveling liquor salesman for a British distillery, peddling Beefeater gin and Haig & Haig scotch to hotels and rumshops across the island.

In front of the property at Runaway Bay was a narrow beach; about a quarter-mile out the water broke on an offshore reef, so that the waves which approached the beach were harmless and slight. At the water's edge the color of the sea was a light blue, by the reef, deep green. Through the light blue shallows Clare could see the almost transparent tendrils of a jellyfish floating near the surface, the mushroom-shaped body languid and apparently lifeless. On her right thigh she had a two-inch scar, long and white, where she had been stung by a jellyfish, a surprise because the animal seemed so incapable of attack. A pink and transparent being carried by the sea, in and then out again, dependent entirely on the movement of the tides, harmless—until a swimmer got too close. On the sand beneath the jellyfish were the distinct spines of a sea egg—also dangerous, but clearly so.

Clare and her father picnicked on the beach that afternoon, and he told her again about the elm trees and how strong and healthy they had been, and about her distinguished ancestor the puisne justice.

Father and daughter drove through the gate of the estate and up the drive toward the great house. It was still standing. Barely standing in the center of the subdivision. A large wooden sign saying PAR-ADISE PLANTATION was propped against the verandah railing, and they could tell that the great house had been left by the developers as a "come on," to convince prospective clients they could buy into the past. Capture history in their summer homes.

In size the house was not really very great—it was low and square, and set on flat ground with a view of the sea in front and the cane-fields in back. It was wooden, with a slightly peaked wooden shingle roof and a wooden verandah marking the perimeter of the building. The wood was bleached almost white—by the sun and the salt breeze from the sea.

"May we go in, Daddy?"

"I don't see why not; after all, it did belong to us once."

So father and daughter climbed the verandah steps and heard the noises of lizards running through the vines and across the lattice-work. Inside the house was dark, and Mr. Savage went back to the car to get a flashlight. His beam scanned the walls and Clare could make out scenes on paper which once had been colored bright red against a white background, now faded pale and darkened by an accumulation of dust. She went closer, and detected that this was a picture—a pattern made of the same picture—of people in a park in a city somewhere in Europe. The women wore long dresses and strolled with their thin-handled parasols unfurled to protect them from the sun. The dresses and parasols were red, the women white. White children played across the paper, and red dogs jumped at sticks. The scene was repeated again and again across the wall; it was not a continuing story with a theme, like the Bayeux tapestry her father had described to her—because, he said, one of her ancestors had fought alongside the Conqueror in 1066. The pattern on the wallpaper was only a small glimpse of the background against which this part of her family had once existed. These images surrounded them as they sat in their parlor. The danger to Clare was that the background could slide so easily into the foreground.

She licked her finger and touched it to the wall, then tasted—it was salt.

"You know, your great-great-grandfather imported all his furnishings from abroad. Settees and tables. Bric-a-brac. Crystal. China. From England and Ireland mostly. Staffordshire. Wedgwood. Waterford. Royal Doulton. Sometimes he brought things out from France and Switzerland. I think this wallpaper must have come from France and the chairs from Switzerland. The rugs came originally from Persia. Fine, fine oriental carpets." Boy Savage was describing, filling in the room for his daughter. The only objects to be seen were a few broken-down chairs stacked in one corner, and these were uninformative as to origin. The flashlight passed over a mantelpiece at the far wall of the parlor—"Carrara marble, from Florence, Italy," her father said. "Over the mantel there used to be a portrait of your great-great-grandmother, painted by a man who had studied with Sir Joshua Reynolds, but it's gone now."

"What happened to it?"

"It was stolen, or got sold; I don't know. It doesn't matter anyway."

The two moved on, into another room behind the parlor, and again the wallpaper caught her eye. This time the scheme was flowers—but no flowers she had ever seen. Foxgloves, bluebells, oxlips, harebells, forget-me-nots, wild roses—once purple, blue, yellow, and pink, now dim—ran across a wall. A pattern of English wildflowers. The paper was torn here and there, and there was nothing but bare white wall underneath.

And so father and daughter walked through what was once a great house, and they came out into the backyard, where the only signs of a former life were the foundation stones of some of the outbuildings, and faint gullies marking the earth where others had been. These buildings out back, only a few yards from the great house, had once contained molasses and rum and slaves—the points of conjunction of the system known as the Triangle Trade. They contained these things and they contained the paraphernalia of day-to-day existence on a sugar plantation. The warehouses held hogsheads and puncheons, barrels in which the sugar and rum were kept. They held billhooks, cutlasses, hoes, axes, shovels—for working the fields and harvesting the cane. Bins of dried beans, sacks of flour and grain, wooden crates of salted herring—these provided the basic diet of the slaves. Salt was important; it compensated sweat. The warehouses held cloth—bolts of blue German linen and coarse red checkered cotton—to make into work clothes for the slaves. Blankets—rough wool—for slaves who took sick, slaves who were lying-in. These things were also imported from England.

The traces in the earth which Clare could now see indicated where the slave cabins had been. Little more than huts, really, twenty to twenty-five feet long and twelve feet wide, made of wattle and plaster, with dirt floors and palm-thatched roofs. Inside, the ceiling was low—usually brushing the forehead—so the inhabitants, if they were any height at all, had to walk stooped forward. As they stooped to hoe; stooped to stir. There were no windows in any of these huts— light in each came from a candle, made with the fat rendered from farm animals. Cool came through the front door, when it was opened. The candle sat on a small table, beside one or two earthenware jars, an iron pot, a pile of calabashes—gourds hollowed out and dried, to be used as plates and cups. The beds were of straw or planks. The lines in the earth were close together, separated only by a few feet, where there might have been a planting of cassava, or yam, or plantain—to supplement the diet provided by the justice.

The outbuildings on which the livelihood of the plantation hinged were these cabins, and the sugar mill and the boiling-house. The cane was cut—after it had reached past the height of a human being—tied into bundles, and carried from the fields to the sugar mill on the backs of cattle or mules or slaves. Inside the mill, huge metal rollers turned slowly; the bundles were passed between the rollers, and the juice was crushed from the stalks of cane. The power which moved the rollers came from wind or water or cattle or mules, or from a tread-mill on which men and women walked. From the sugar mill the juice flowed along an open pipe—a large open pipe made of mahogany or bamboo—to the boiling-house, where the liquid was clarified in huge copper cauldrons, sitting on woodfires fed by the refuse of the cane—nothing was wasted. The heat of the boiling-house was intense, as the steam from the liquid filled the atmosphere, radiating from the brick walls and the metal vats. Slaves ladled the purified juice from the cauldrons and filled the flat cooling trays which sat on a shelf by the windows of the boiling-house.

At the surface of the trays, the sugar crystallized. Beneath the crys-tal surface, the molasses remained liquid. The sugar was skimmed away and packed into barrels. The molasses was treated to become rum. Each product was then transported to Port Antonio or Montego Bay, and thence shipped to Great Britain.

From the backyard, in which she now stood, noting the existence of the foundation stones and the gullies in the earth, but not knowing the former life they represented, Clare could see in the distance long funnels of smoke and an occasional tongue of flame. The Paradise Plantation was burning the canefields to clear the land and begin con-struction of the vacation homes.

⌒

There had been no cataclysm in Jamaica; no bloody Civil War to end involuntary servitude. The end of slavery was a decision on the part of Her Majesty's government, after decades of consideration and decades of guerrilla warfare. And, of course, the growing Victorian desire for West African palm oil. One soap manufacturer, in the city of Manchester, had a sign in his shop window which highlighted this particular development: BUY OUR PALM OIL SOAP AND CON-TRIBUTE TO THE ABOLITION OF SLAVERY. Clear and to the point—the perfect Victorian marriage of economy and altruism.

Sugar depended on slavery to survive. When abolition finally came in 1834, the sugar industry suffered a reversal from which it never completely recovered. Three hundred acres was the minimum expanse of land a sugar plantation could measure—in order to make a profit. One slave was required for every two acres—compared to one slave for every five or ten acres on a cotton plantation. This estimate takes into account the fact that the slaves would be worked twelve hours a day and six days a week. At least.

Sugar was never a very profitable enterprise. It required an unending supply of unpaid labor—even with this labor supply, sugar plantations turned only the most minimal profits. But sugar was a necessity of western civilization—to the tea-drinkers of England and the coffee-drinkers on the Continent, those who used it to sweeten their beverage, or who laced these beverages with rum. Those who took these products at their leisure—to finish a meal, begin a day, to stimulate them, keep them awake, as they considered fashion or poetry or politics or family, sitting around their cherrywood tables or relaxing in their wingback chairs. People who spent afternoons in the clubs of Mayfair or evenings in the cafés on the rue de la Paix. People holding forth in Parliament. The Rathaus. The Comedie Française. People who talked revolution or who worried about revolution. They took their coffee and tea, their sugar and rum, from trays held by others, as their cotton was milled by others, and their lands were kept by others. The fabric of their society, their civilization, their culture, was an intricate weave, at the heart of which was enforced labor of one kind or another.

Slavery was not an aberration—it was an extreme. Consider the tea plantations of Ceylon and China. The coffee plantations of Sumatra and Colombia. The tobacco plantations of Pakistan and the Philippines. The mills of Lowell. Manchester. Leeds. Marseilles. The mines of Wales, Alsace-Lorraine. The railroads of the Union-Pacific. Cape-to-Cairo. All worked by captive labor.

To some this may be elementary—but it is important to take it all in, the disconnections and the connections, in order to understand the limits of the abolition of slavery. The enslavement of Black people— African peoples—with its processions of naked and chained human beings, whipping of human beings, rape of human beings, lynching of human beings, buying and selling of human beings—made other forms of employment in the upkeep of western civilization seem pale. So slavery-in-fact—which was distasteful to some of the coffee-drinkers and tea-drinkers, who might have read about these things or saw them illustrated in the newspapers the clubs and cafés provided for their patrons, neatly hung on a rack from dowel sticks—

slavery-in-fact was abolished, and the freedom which followed on abolition turned into veiled slavery, the model of the rest of the western world.

When slavery-in-fact ended and the slaves on the plantation became freedmen and freedwomen, the sugar industry collapsed. The planters mortgaged their properties to keep going, but the Bank of England foreclosed on many of them and their loans were called in. Piece by piece these landowners went under. The Crown paid nineteen pounds in cash compensation to the landowners for each freed slave, but many investors had gone into debt buying slaves for far more than that amount.

There was no cash compensation for the people who had labored under slavery. No tracts of land for them to farm. No employment for the most part. No literacy programs. No money to book passage back to Africa. Their enslavement had become an inconvenience—and now it was removed. All the forces which worked to keep these people slaves now worked to keep them poor. And poor most of them remained.

In the Savage family, none of this was ever mentioned. None of these details were touched upon. The family's loss of wealth was put on the reputation of one individual—Mr. Levi, a Jew who was hired as an estate manager in 1845, eleven years after these events were set in motion. The Savages were possessed of an arrogance which seemed to grow in relation to their losses—no longer threatening, when they became poor, their arrogance became to some, pathetic—like a man panhandling in an evening suit. To others, because of the family name and general coloration, their arrogance was still a force, a power once specific, now abstract—there were some who would turn to the man in the evening suit and ask him the time, even though they knew he had pawned his watch long since. According to their arrogance, the Savages saw themselves as blameless for any downward turn in their fortunes. They managed to relinquish responsibility for their lives. This arrogance, and their failures, bred a paranoia among the Savages, which was passed down through the family as a "logical distrust" of anyone not like them. And there were so few like them.

The definition of what a Savage was like was fixed by color, class, and religion, and over the years a carefully contrived mythology was constructed, which they used to protect their identities. When they were poor, and not all of them white, the mythology persisted. They swore by it. It added a depth to their conversation, and kept them interested in each other. Only in each other. If the conversation turned to the knotty hair of a first cousin, it would be switched to the Savage ancestor who had been the first person to publically praise *Paradise Lost*. If the too-dark skin of a newborn baby was in question, it would be countered with the life of a Savage who had "done his duty" onboard the *H. M. S. Victory* with Nelson at Trafalgar. If someone spoke about cousin so-and-so being mistaken for "colored," someone else would bring out the snuffbox carved from the Rock of Gibraltar, given to a titled Savage—a lady-in-waiting, it was said, at Queen Victoria's Court. In this way the Savages were hard put to explain the changes in their complexions, eyes, hair, and why so many of them had freckles. They were emphatic in their statement that James Edward Constable Savage, the puisne justice and advisor to the Crown, who had studied law at the Inns of Court, had been one of the only Jamaican landowners never to impregnate a female slave or servant—that is not to say, of course, that he never raped one. To cope in their minds with the absence of his wife, and his resulting needs, the Savages talked of a dark Guatemalan mistress, part Indian, with some Spanish blood, who appeared to them as the personification of the New World. They wanted to forget about Africa.

But they did not pretend that J. E. C. Savage had been a benign slaveholder—they talked of his treatment of runaways, if recaptured, and took some family pride that he administered the punishment himself. The recaptured slave was strung up in front of the quarters, where the queen's justice applied the cat-o'-nine tails to his or her back. The number of lashes depended upon the exertion the justice was capable of on a given afternoon, or morning. Usually about a hundred or so strokes. After the whipping, the slave had salt rubbed into the wounds on his or her back. Then the slave was hanged by the neck until dead, from the large silk cotton tree in the backyard. Finally the rebel was cut down and the justice dissected the naked body of the African man or woman into four parts. Each quadrant of this human body was suspended by rope from a tree at a corner of the property, where it stayed until the vultures, called John Crows, or the bluebottle flies finished it off. They ate the flesh and the blood. The bones fell to the ground where they melded with the earth, fertilizing the cane with potash.

Clare had been taught at St. Catherine's School for Girls that Jamaica had been a slave society. The white and creole mistresses hastened to say that England was the first country to free its slaves. They also taught her about Anne Bonney and Mary Reade, the pirates. Captain Kidd. Henry Morgan, a buccaneer who had become governor. Port Royal, the meeting place for galleons and privateers on the Spanish Main, which sank under the sea in an earthquake in the seventeenth century as payment for its wickedness. She learned that there had been a freedmen's uprising at Morant Bay in 1865, led by Paul Bogle; but that this rebellion had been unwarranted and of little consequence, and that Bogle had been rightfully executed by the governor. She knew that there had been Maroons, and that many of them still existed in the towns of the Cockpit Country. But she learned that these towns had been a gift from England in compensation for slavery. Slaves mixed with pirates. Revolution with reward. And a sense of history was lost in romance. This history was slight compared to the history of Empire. The politics of freedmen paled beside the politics of commonwealth.

The Savages' standing took its final downslide—rapidly—when Boy's grandfather, James Arthur Constable, took over. J. A. C. Savage, called Jack, traveled to Cambridge University, Clare College, where he read classics. When he returned to the island, he possibly had convinced himself of his dinner-party conversations in England—in which he had presented himself as the heir to great fortunes. But his father, the justice, had begun selling off his estates long before Jack left for Cambridge; by the time Jack returned, only three of the seven plantations remained.

Jack became disheartened when he contemplated what this meant in terms of his future, and he established his life into a daily pattern: leatherbound copies of Ovid and Plato, beside crystal decanters of rum. He began every day by opening a rum bottle—rather, by having it opened for him—and having it poured into a crystal decanter, and thence into a crystal goblet. It was rum from his own sugar cane, aged in wooden kegs, and poured into dark brown bottles bearing the name SAVAGE and the motto from the family crest: MIHI SOLICITUDO FUTURI—TO ME THE CARE OF THE FUTURE.

Jack drank his rum and read his Greek and Latin until he fell asleep. The justice eventually died of old age, and Jack married late— a woman of similar background named Isabel Frazier. She was dark, with green eyes, and thick dark hair that waved to her waist. Together they moved to the last plantation the Savages owned, overlooking the cove of Dry Harbor—so named by Columbus in 1503 when he docked there and found no fresh water to replenish his ship's stores.

Jack and Isabel had six children—five daughters and a son, the youngest child. They lived by selling off the property piece by piece, so that by the time their son was born they only had the house and the outbuildings, and one acre square around. By now, Jack Savage bought his rum from a rumshop—and his books were beginning to crack at the spine.

It was at this time, according to the Savage family chronicles, that Jack decided to make back his fortunes. He purchased a racehorse on credit, which he named Curzon, after the viceroy of India. He trained the horse himself, and found a small Black man who was willing to ride for him. Then Jack contacted a Syrian businessman who was willing to put up ten thousand pounds as a wager that his horse, Khayaam, could beat Curzon.

On a Saturday afternoon at Knutsford Park, the racetrack in Kingston, Jack set his horse against the Syrian's Khayaam in a mile and a quarter race. It was over quickly—Curzon fell in the stretch, Khayaam trampled the jockey, and Jack took his pistol and blew out his horse's brains. He handed over the remains of his estate to the businessman and went to the racetrack stewards to lodge an official protest that the "blasted Arab" had doped his horse. The stewards listened and then offered Jack a tent for his family and a space in the paddock where they could pitch it. This was the low point.

Jack sat under the flap of canvas with his last bottle of rum and raged against the "damned Arab," the "damned nigger," and the "idiot stewards." He was a classicist, and so he thought of Achilles sulking in his tent during the Trojan War—and of the uncontrollable temper of the Greek hero. It was Isabel who interrupted his thoughts and suggested that they telegraph the jockey's wife to tell her what had happened to her husband. She was not literate, but perhaps the minister of her church would read the news to her.

"Damned sweet of you, Isabel; always thinking about the niggers. Damned sweet."

Jack knew even in his reverie that his family could not live forever in a racetrack compound; so he set off for Alaska to mine gold, and then headed for the Panama Canal, where he managed to get work as an overseer of the diggers.

There he died of yellow fever, although the family insisted that he had been bitten by some exotic snake.

Back in the car, sun glaring through the front window in the hot afternoon, sea beside them, still, aquamarine. Driving toward Ocho Rios, where her father had an appointment with the manager of the Arawak Hotel, Clare thought about the great house. The time which had passed through it. The salt taste of the walls. She sometimes imagined that the walls of certain places were the records of those places—the events which happened there. More accurate than the stories of the people who had lived within the walls. She did not remember where she had gotten this idea, but she held on to it. The walls might not be able to reveal exactly what they had seen, but perhaps they could indicate to a visitor something, if only a clue, about the time which had passed through them. Maybe there were signs marked on the walls each time they heard a shout—like the slashes on the Rosetta Stone, which she had learned about in school.

She tried to think of the walls in the house and what she could remember from them. They were already dimming in her mind. She began to confuse the ladies on the paper with the women in her past. Lace. Parasols. Wide skirts. Heads bent in discretion and secrets. Clare assumed the women who had lived in the great house had been as white as the women on the paper.

Chapter Five

Inez, the woman the justice had taken to be his mistress, was bronze. Her mother was a half-blood Miskito Indian, whose people had come from the mountain chain of Central America. Her father was a Maroon, an Ashanti from the Gold Coast. Inez was known as a friend of the slaves on the Savage Plantation. Her mother's ancestors had been among the Indians the Red Coats brought to the island to defeat the armies of the Maroons. But they went over to the Maroon side—lived among them, and married with them. Her father and mother settled in the Cockpit Country near to Trelawny Town and kept a small farm, trading with other Maroon people and with the few settlements of poor whites and creoles nearby.

It was night in the parlor. The moon came through the windows which she kept open to catch the salt breeze—when the judge returned, he would latch them again, saying that the air would damage his wallpaper and his furniture. And he had a fear of the slaves watching him while he read—but he did not mention this. Inez sat with the moonlight behind her and a lighted candle shaded at her side. The sofa was made of heavy tufted cloth, designed with gold threads which crossed over each other; the justice had ordered it from Geneva, he said. She sat there with a book in her hand—the poetry of Lord Byron—she was teaching herself to read while the judge was away. On the floor a Persian carpet was laid, a thick weave on which bright royal blue peacocks strutted across the parlor. Over the marble mantelpiece was a picture hung in a gilt frame—a portrait of the judge's wife-in-England: a young woman whose face was framed in curls, her hands folded in her lap, wearing lace and brocade, a bouquet of white roses beside her.

The justice was in Kingston, bringing a petition from the planters on the North Coast to try and stop the bill of emancipation.

Inez was not officially a slave—she had not been placed naked on an auction block, her teeth had not been marveled at by a prospective buyer. The judge found her in his courtroom one morning, brought up on charges of the theft of a rifle and some ammunition from the Selby Plantation. Her father had need of a gun—to hunt and for protection—some of the white and creole settlers were being troublesome, and had begun to poach animals from their farm. So Inez was sent to St. Ann to fetch one for him from a slave who was an ally of the Maroons. But she had been caught on the path leading away from the estate—someone must have informed; it happened. Some damn *quashee*, thinking freedom would be his or hers in exchange for information. Massa Selby brought her into the courtroom, where she would have had her hands cut off at the wrists, or been given a hundred strokes of the cat, but the judge intervened and took her home, where he raped her. He raped her for six weeks until he left on one of his trips to London. She was eighteen.

Now she was twenty. She had survived by planning her escape, waiting for emancipation, devising a way to avenge herself—all of these things. She had been taught the ways of her mother's people and the ways of the Maroons, and she made spells with feathers and stones and shells and tried to work her way out. There was a slave-woman in the quarters whom she visited and who taught her more about *obeah* and magic. This woman's name was Mma Alli—a strange woman with a right breast that had never grown. She said she was a one-breasted warrior woman and represented a tradition which was older than the one which had enslaved them. She said she was one of the very few of her kind in the New World. Where in some places Mma Alli might have been shunned or cast out or made fun of, the slaves on the Savage Plantation respected her greatly. The women came to her with their troubles, and the men with their pain. She gave of her time and her secrets. She counseled how to escape—and when. She taught the children the old ways—the knowledge she brought from Africa—and told them never to forget them and to carry them on. She described the places they had all come from, where one-breasted women were bred to fight.

Mma Alli had never lain with a man. The other slaves said she loved only women in that way, but that she was a true sister to the men—the Black men: her brothers. They said that by being with her in bed, women learned all manner of the magic of passion. How to become wet again and again all through the night. How to soothe and excite at the same time. How to touch a woman in her deep-inside and make her womb move within her. She taught many of the women on the plantation about this passion and how to take strength from it. To keep their bodies as their own, even while they were made subject to the whimsical violence of the justice and his slavedrivers, who were for the most part creole or *quashee*.

When Inez came to Mma Alli to get rid of the mixed-up baby she carried, Mma Alli kept her in her cabin overnight. She brewed a tea of roots and leaves, said a Pawpaw chant over it, and when it was beginning to take effect and Inez was being rocked by the contractions of her womb, Mma Alli began to gently stroke her with fingers dipped in coconut oil and pull on her nipples with her mouth, and the thick liquid which had been the mixed-up baby came forth easily and Inez felt little pain. A baby, Inez's people believed, was sacred, but a baby conceived in *buckra* rape would have no soul—with this Mma Alli agreed. Her tongue all over Inez's body—night after night—until the judge returned from his trip to London and Inez had to return to the great house. But she went there with a newfound power.

With Mma Alli she remembered her mother and her people and knew she would return home.

Inez took a square of Irish linen from the judge's trunk, and pulled some long strands of her blue-black hair free from her braid. With a small knife she cut through the strands, threaded a needle, and embroidered a picture on the cloth for Mma Alli. The outline of an orchid—the plant she knew from the Cockpits, suspended in the green of the crevasses, living on air and water. And also light. She drew her needle through the pale, loosely woven fibers and traced the lip of the flower with her hair. She thickened her stitches to reveal where the orifice hid behind the ridges of the orchid's tongue. Storing its honeyed juice for the night-flying moths that sought the flower during the full moon.

She mixed colors in calabashes—taking red from clay, blue from indigo, yellow from arsenic—and with her knife, sharpened bamboo splints. At the end of the splints she fixed some pieces of sponge from the sea, and working slowly, filled in the outline she had drawn, a keepsake for the walls of Mma Alli's cabin, to be placed alongside the *abeng* which Mma Alli kept oiled with coconut and suspended from a piece of sisal and a fishhook.

⌒

The great house had seemed so small, Clare thought. Broken down. The house was not at all what she had expected. It was as though she had wanted it to be a time machine rather than a relic. A novel rather than an obituary. She wanted to know the people who had lived there. The people she had been given an idea of. Men with swords and carriages—horses imported from Arabia and wine from the Rhine Valley. That was what she imagined. People who came from "England," that place she knew from her father's stories and her teachers' lessons. Where everyone was civilized and no one had to be told which fork to use. England was their mother country. *Everyone* there was white, her teachers told her. Jamaica was the "prizest" possession of the Crown, she had read in her history book. And she had been told that there was a special bond between this still-wild island and that perfect place across the sea.

England was where Charles Dickens had come from. They were studying him in school, reading his novel *Great Expectations*. She liked

Pip and he reminded her of herself in some ways. She occasionally lived with people other than her parents—she spent her school vacations with her grandmother, and other times, when things were not "going well" between her mother and father, she stayed with their friends or relatives in town. Sometimes she felt sure that she would make her own way in the world—would "be" someone, as Pip had wanted for himself. And it bothered her that she would probably have to leave this place—her family's island—in order to achieve anything. England. America. These were the places island people went to get ahead.

The idea of a benefactor captured her—and she wondered who her benefactor would be. The convict or the unmarried woman. The Black or the white. Both perhaps. Her father told her she was white. But she knew that her mother was not. Who would she choose were she given the choice: Miss Havisham or Abel Magwitch? She was of both dark and light. Pale and deeply colored. To whom would she turn if she needed assistance? From who would she expect it? Her mother or her father—it came down to that sometimes. Would her alliances shift at any given time.

The Black or the white? A choice would be expected of her, she thought.

She thought about Pip now because the great house reminded her of Miss Havisham's room. Dingy and mindful of the past. Both the source of her and not the source of her. The house carried over to her a sense of great disappointment—maybe of great sadness. It was a dry and dusty place—not a place of her dreams. She felt a sense of loss and betrayal. Not the matter of a bridegroom missing his wedding. Her teacher had taught her that Miss Havisham had a broken heart, and that women used to die of broken hearts. White English women who had suffered great disappointment. The house did not have a broken heart. Did houses have hearts at all?

She had had expectations of the great house. Now—she wished that the fire in the canefields would spread to the house and that it would burn down to the ground. She didn't need the house, now she had seen it. If it burned, only the stories she knew would be left. The white ladies on the wall would be laid to rest—the residue of salt on the paper would spark blue when the fire reached it.

But the great house never burned to the ground. It was spruced up and made into a flagship for the Paradise Plantation. Fitted with period furniture imported from a factory in Massachusetts which made replicas of antiques. And white plaster dummies from a factory in New York City, which supplied several Fifth Avenue department stores, were dressed in nineteenth-century costume, and placed on the verandah and through the rooms. One larger-than-life white dummy was dressed like an overseer, with a cat-o'-nine tails in one plaster fist, and a wide-brimmed straw hat on his head. He stood firmly, with his legs apart, to the side of the great house, welcoming purchasers to the subdivision.

A small patch of canefield was left by the developers. And Black Jamaicans, also in period costume—but alive, not replicas—were paid to stand around with machetes and hoes, and give directions to interested parties.

The brochure stressed "atmosphere."

There had once been a fire at Runaway Bay, but it had never touched the great house.

The night the justice returned to the plantation from Kingston, where his petition had been a failure, he walked up the verandah steps and came into the parlor—but Inez was nowhere to be found. He sat heavily on the tufted sofa and waited, the mud from the journey flecking the peacocks beneath his feet. But she did not return. He poured himself a draught of rum and thought with astonishment and disgust about the fact—now it *was* a fact—that his slaves would be free in a matter of months. The justice worried what would happen to the island when it swarmed with free Africans, some only a few years out of the bush. Who would have conceived that the empire would see fit to unleash these people. The justice was not thinking about his crops or even the future of his properties. His mind was on a "higher" plane—he was concerned about the survival of his race. He was fearful of the mixing which was sure to follow freedom—in which the white seed would be diluted and the race impoverished. He thought along the lines of Jefferson and Franklin, the founding fathers of a free society of white men—both of these, Virginian and Yankee, enlightened thinkers, had written letters and tracts warning about the danger to the white race once Black blood mingled with it. Franklin had written that of all the people of the earth, only the English and the German Saxons represented the purity and superiority of the white race—the pinnacle of human life. The judge had read Franklin's words more than once:

And while we are . . . *Scouring* our planet, by clearing America of Woods, and so making this Side of our Globe reflect a brighter Light to the Eyes of Inhabitants in Mars or Venus, why should we in the Sight of Superior Beings, darken its People?

To have a notion of Black freedmen, the justice thought, would be like wearing a garment—he searched his mind for an analogy—a garment dipped in the germs of the plague. Yet there were children on the plantation, as there were on Jefferson's plantation, who were of the judge—his offspring—but these were not his heirs, these were his property. And he had sent children like these to the slave market in Kingston more than once.

With this heaviness the judge stalked to the quarters calling for Inez. It is very important to note here that although the judge had had a drink of rum, he was cold sober. His mind was moving through a logical series of suppositions and conclusions informed by his beliefs and his assessment of experience. He lit a torch from the kitchen fire and called the name of the woman he had raped again and again. He approached the cabin of Mma Alli when there was no answer to his calls.

"Inez not in here, Massa Justice. Me no know where him be." Mma Alli poked her head out the cabin door.

"You know everything that goes on on this plantation, bitch; tell me where my nigger wench is."

"Me not know, sah."

Inez had made her move that afternoon. Back to the Cockpits. Meeting with the slaves on the plantation, all had decided that after freedom—and they knew that freedom was coming; there were spies in the households of the governor and some of the members of the island's assembly—after freedom they would have no certainty of employment, no guarantee that there would be peace between the former slaveowners and the former slaves. Someone even suggested that they shouldn't have to work for these men after freedom—"Me would preffer starve." Someone else said she thought their goal after freedom should be to return to Africa. To achieve this, she continued, would mean "getting us some land and saving monies for our passage back." It was agreed that whether their aim be to stay and make a life for themselves on the island or to save and return to Africa, they needed property of their own. Inez had returned to the Cockpits to find the mayor of Trelawny Town and speak to him on behalf of the slaves on the Savage Plantation about getting a piece of land for them to farm together after freedom. She took some gold sovereigns from the strongbox beside the judge's desk as partial payment for the property and tools. She did not expect to come back to Runaway Bay—she would send word to the slaves about the results of her petition.

The judge's anger rose with each denial he met from each one of the slaves he questioned—"Me no know, Massa." "Me know not, Massa." "Me nebber se de gal, Massa Justice."

Later, he would look back on what he had done and assess that he was a man of passion who had been pushed to his limit. His passion had been misled to violence. He was not to blame. These people were slaves and would not know how to behave in freedom. They would have been miserable. He was a justice: he had been trained to assess the alternatives available to human beings, and their actions within the limits of these alternatives. These people were not equipped to cope with the responsibilities of freedom. These people were Africans. Their parameters of behavior were out of the range of civilized men. Their lives obviously of less value. They had been brought here for one purpose, and one purpose only—and this was about to be removed. Even more than the papist Irish he had once assessed for the Crown, the dark people existed on another, lower level of being. He believed all this absolutely. And he held that among these people life was cheap, and death did not matter. His conclusion was far from original among his own kind: At that moment these people were his property, and they were therefore his to burn.

Not all died that night; some escaped into the interior of the island and managed to find Inez. There she was waiting for them with land and tools. They told her that the fire began at the cabin of Mma Alli and that the old warrior woman—their strict teacher and true sister—had been trapped as the flames caught the thatch and the tightly woven palm collapsed inward.

Lest anyone think the judge's action—which became the pattern of foundation stones and thin dirt gullies Clare saw that afternoon behind the great house, rectangles remembering an event she would never know of—lest anyone think the judge's behavior extreme or insane or frenzied, the act of a mad white man, it should be pointed out that this was not an isolated act on the eve of African freedom in Jamaica.

The bones of dead slaves made the land at Runaway Bay rich and green. Tall royal palms lined the avenues leading to the houses of the development. Breadfruit trees, branches fat with their deep green lobed leaves, created shades around the stucco bungalows. The breeze from the sea came through the windows of the houses and made the walls taste of salt.

Chapter Six

Mr. Savage's car, a 1956 Morris Minor convertible, passed by Dunn's River Falls, a series of cascades which poured into the sea at Ocho Rios. They stopped briefly to watch a group of children slide through the falls on banana leaves, down the rocks flattened into slopes by the water.

Jack Savage's second youngest daughter, Caroline, was the mother of Boy. In 1921, when she was a young woman, she made the journey to America, to New York City, to make her way as an actress. To "go on the stage," as the expression went. Almost on her arrival, through another Jamaican daughter-turned-actress, she landed a job in the chorus of *Shuffle Along*, where, unknown to her family, Caroline passed herself off as a "high yaller." But, in fact, that is exactly what she was. Through her mother, Isabel.

Caroline made a catch-as-catch-can living on the stage, and became involved with someone she would describe in her letters to her family as a stage-door johnny, a man who courted her in tails and with small bouquets of Parma violets, but who actually was an iceman from Sicily, who serviced the boarding house in Hell's Kitchen where she lodged. With the iceman she had Boy, to whom she gave her surname. She did not marry the iceman, saying to herself that she could not marry beneath her "station"; for her family she invented a car crash in which the stage-door johnny's roadster—a 1920 Bugatti—flipped over on a curve near 86th Street in Central Park, breaking her intended's neck as he raced to his wedding with Caroline.

In fact, the iceman had been deported to Sicily because of some difficulty with his passport, so he said. Caroline faced up to her fate, though, and the other showgirls, who kept a fund for such troubles, offered to cover the cost of an abortion and gave Caroline the name of a doctor on Jane Street. They were surprised when Caroline refused, saying that this was not something she could ever bring herself to do—the family line was too important to be broken. Why, some of the greatest men in history had been bastards. She named a few names and the showgirls gave her money for her confinement instead. Caroline had her baby in a rest home in Hoboken, New Jersey, stayed with him for a few months, and then sent him to her sister Henrietta in Old Harbour, who had offered to raise him for a time. Boy did not travel unaccompanied—there was always some Jamaican returning home willing to watch over another Jamaican's child. Caroline found a nice young woman whom she gave a few dollars extra and the trainfare to Old Harbour.

Caroline wrote to her son occasionally, sending him programs and clippings describing her place in the American theater, and he waited for her to send for him—"when I'm settled." He knew his mother as a beautiful dark-haired woman with long showgirl-stockinged legs, who sent him books for Christmas and his birthday without fail. He longed for her and built his longings around the Great White Way and Tin Pan Alley, places she described to him, and tried to visualize life with his mother there. But soon there came news that she was ill in Hollywood, where she had gone to break into the talkies, and later, that she was dead of something or other. Boy never forgot her.

Henrietta and her husband, Archie, were drunks. Not mean drunks, just sodden and soppy alcoholics. He trained racehorses and she sewed jockeys' silks. When they won, they drank, and bought drinks all around. When they lost, they bought liquor on credit.

Henrietta and Archie talked all day and all night of family. Of the history of family. Of the need for roots and the knowledge of where you came from. And they emphasized their philosophy of family with tales of the Savages. They were not unkind people at all—they were silly people, who removed themselves from any sense of reality and became lost in a myth which they believed. They were people for whom the possibilities of the future lay in the next horserace or the next drink—these were the things around which their existences pivoted and their decisions were made. And Henrietta and Archie, through

their hazes and hangovers, gave depth to this way of being by recon-
structing the past.

Boy became their adopted son after the death of Caroline. He had
inherited his mother's beauty—black, almost blue, hair. Curly hair. And
green-green eyes. He had a large, distinguished nose, the mark of the
iceman. And he was bright as well as beautiful—he spent much of his
time alone, reading the books his mother had sent him and imagining
about what he read. There were no other children near the small house
at the back of the racetrack where he lived with his aunt and uncle, at
least no children with whom he was allowed to play. And in his soli-
tude he created Camelot and Pompeii, imagined the Charge of the
Light Brigade and Custer's Last Stand, crossed the Khyber Pass and
wrenched Excalibur from the stone.

When he was ten years old, Boy won a scholarship to a Jesuit
boarding school in Brownstown, in the center of the island. There
he attached himself to the priests, who were taken in both by his
beauty and his devotion to study. Under the priests, Boy turned from
chivalry and exploration to the legends of the saints, the miracles of
Fatima and Lourdes, the records of stigmata—all the romance of
Catholicism. These spiraled into the major passion of his youth—the
Shroud of Turin. This piece of linen cloth became the backdrop which
shadowed several years of his life. And for a long time afterward,
during the war, as a married man, as a professional Calvinist finally,
Boy thought about the shroud and what it might mean—what was its
secret.

In the study of the priest in charge of religious training, Father
Gregory, Boy found a book by a French surgeon, Pierre Barbet, enti-
tled *A Doctor at Calvary*. In his experience with amputated limbs and
lifeless bodies, the doctor became equipped to solve the mystery of
the shroud—whether it was authentic, whether it revealed all the
wounds of Jesus. His book was a detailed medical account of each as-
sault on the body of a man imprinted on the long winding sheet,
which was concealed above the main altar of a church in Turin. The
doctor carefully and painstakingly analyzed all the puncture marks
of the corpse which had been wrapped in the shroud, at one point
hanging himself on a cross to test his theories of crucifixion. The nails
had been driven through the wristbones, he concluded. The body had
been chastised by a *flagrum*—the whip the Romans used on the backs
of slaves—at least a hundred times. The wound at the side of the

victim had drained the heart of blood, and so brought on death sooner than was usual—a mercy killing. The traces of blood from the heart of this man were still to be found on the cloth. Boy took all of these details into himself and argued with the Jesuits that this cloth was the only true relic of Christendom. If this seemed to the priests a childish passion, it was childish only in the innocence with which their pupil approached the possibility of the shroud. His passion was as strong as any adult passion.

As he got older, in his teens, Boy did not so much focus on the nature of the shroud as the burial cloth of a tortured human being. He made his focus the flash of light which he believed fixed the image to the cloth when the soul of the dead man left the body. He imagined the soul moving outward into space to be united with the source of all. His understanding of the essence of life as something conceived and controlled by an extraterrestrial force may have begun here. Caroline had moved outward into space. So had Jesus. He took great comfort in this relic stored in several caskets—of wood, iron, asbestos, silver—wrapped in silk and velvet and locked behind a metal grille in an Italian church. This was magic. This was what life was all about.

The magic was also contained in Stonehenge—Boy puzzled about the transportation of the monoliths across the Irish Sea by the Druids. It was contained in the Pyramids of Egypt and the temple of Angkor. These structures were connected to another place, as well as another time. Almost everywhere he looked, Boy perceived the supernatural nature of existence. And where many people will admit that there is a supernatural aspect to human existence, that the entire reality of life is supernatural, in the sense of being mysterious and unexplained, they protect themselves from this knowledge rather than confronting it—confronting it will yield them no comfort—and they couch their terror in religious dogma and ways to pass the time. Boy did not turn from religious dogma, but he kept to the magical, expanding his sense of it, and left the mundane to others. He courted rather than denied the supernatural, and somehow took comfort in a force outside himself which was responsible for all. He briefly entertained the thought that Jesus, in reality, was a visitor from another planet, and that his beloved shroud proved, with its photographic imprint, the swift departure of Christ to another world.

In his early life, Boy thought about joining the priesthood, or entering a monastery, where the notions he held could be contemplated for a lifetime. He would be taken care of, with a small rectangular room holding him, and the Church attending to his every need. But then the war came, and he was drafted into the British forces along with thousands of other colonials. He was assigned to the 8th Army and spent some time in North Africa, crossing back and forth across sand dunes in pursuit of the Desert Fox, one Nazi for whom the British claimed great respect. Boy's immediate commander in the Sahara was a Scottish sergeant who taught him how to drink, and taught him an appreciation of Calvinism. In the cool of the desert at night the sergeant lectured to any and all who would listen about the stark practices of the Presbyterian Church. It was the concept of the Elect which held Boy's attention—the Elect—those whose names were recorded before time. Those who no matter what they did or did not do were the only saved souls on earth. The ones who had been chosen. Life here and now was proved to be nothing—it was the afterlife which was real, in which all would be beautiful, pure, white. This he came to believe, and this kept him going. His name was on some otherworldly roll and would never be erased, while other poor bastards whose names were not writ large would try and try to achieve the status he had been born to. Let the country people talk about the life everlasting. Let Brother Emmanuel promise his congregation deliverance. Let Miss Mattie and her circle speak of redemption. None of these would know the sweetness of eternity—they were not chosen.

Throughout his life Boy insisted that the Jesuits had set him down on the right track with regard to education and the pursuit of his unknown God. This group of Black and white and creole priests, faithful to a man they called the Black Pope, the general of their order, also taught Boy to respect elitism—and that there was no shame in being an exception. The Jesuits themselves, after all, were divine exceptions, and it sometimes seemed that the strict canon of the Church could not contain their brilliance. Boy took pride in this. Thinking he had been born an exception, he set out to earn no distinctions at all.

Even though he traded Jesuit Catholicism for the bare bones of Calvinism, Boy kept a special place in his heart for the priests. Why not. He didn't practice Calvinism in his day-to-day life—that sort of ascetic devotion was for the unsaved, the unexceptional, who might hope to be scribbled in the margins of the great book. Boy only had to wait for the moment when the record of the Elect would be opened and his name would be revealed alongside the names of other Savages. Kept safe by the Puritan Almighty with the power to transport souls into space.

Little of this was articulated by Boy to any but his elder daughter. She was a true Savage, he assured her. Her fate was sealed.

⁓

In 1945, after VE Day, Boy returned to Jamaica, where he met Kitty Freeman, who had spent the war years in the British consul's office in Washington, D.C. They married against great opposition from Kitty's family, and Clare was born soon after.

Eva falla-line gal
Eva run come back
Eva
Eva falla-line gal
Eva run come back
Eva
Eva falla-line gal
Eva run come back
What I gwan to do wit' dat falla-line gal
Eva, oh, Eva.

Eva walk go a Kingston
Eva run come back
Eva
Eva walk go a Kingston
Eva run come back
Eva
Eva walk go a Kingston
Eva run come back
What I gwan to do wit' dat falla-line gal
Eva, oh, Eva.

Dem put Eva inna bed
Eva could not sleep
Eva
Dem put Eva inna bed
Eva could not sleep
Eva
Dem put Eva inna bed
Eva could not sleep
Put her on de floor
Eva sleep like angel
Eva, oh, Eva.

—traditional.

Chapter Seven

Clare usually spent August and September at her grandmother's house, while her sister was sent to another relative, and their parents remained in Kingston. But in and out of the year, the family traveled between St. Elizabeth and Kingston, bringing back to town things from country, and bringing to country things from town. These two distinct places created the background for the whole of their existence. And the places reflected the separate needs and desires of the two parents. It seemed to Clare that Kitty came alive only in the bush, while Boy armed himself against it, carrying newspapers and books and liquor, and a Swiss watch to mark off the time. Town was evil, Kitty held—people taken from country couldn't survive there. The tin-and-cloth shanties were proof of this—the children with no teeth and big bellies and the sad-looking women who walked back and forth between the shanties and the standpipes, that space being the limits of their movement, were living proof. Boy avoided the shanties as much as he could, trying to keep his daily progress between the hotels and the racetracks.

The daughters' lives were bound, as are the lives of most children, by the personalities of their parents, and the events of their lives, the way the car took as they drove between country and town, were dictated by the needs and desires of these two people. Which is of course nothing new—only something which makes resistance very difficult, and may even make a child believe that resistance is impossible or unnecessary.

As Clare and her father and mother and sister were driving down the mountain away from her grandmother's house and toward town, it grew dark. It was late on a Saturday evening and they had been delayed in their departure by a rainstorm. A quick downpour which first appeared as dark clouds over the mountain's run and moved into the valley in a matter of minutes.

Ahead of them now, winding down the road, was a procession of people dressed in white, their presences lit by the torches they all carried. Soft drink and Red Stripe beer bottles had been filled with kerosene and lit from a rag wick stuffed inside. The people marched in pairs. In the middle of the procession were four men, each holding in his hands the end of a freshly cut green bamboo pole that rose about three feet from each man's shoulder. Between the four poles a hammock swung in the night breeze, which was by now dry and cool. The hammock was made from a white sheet, and it dipped and swayed in the middle as the procession moved forward.

"What are those people carrying?" Clare asked.

Her mother answered her. "It is a funeral procession. Someone has died, God rest his soul, and they are taking the body to a service."

The procession moved forward underneath a steady hum, which at first seemed of the same key and pitch, but soon differentiated into harmony, led by the high falsetto of a man, whose voice circled the hum and turned it into a mourning chant. The words of the chant were strange, unrecognizable.

"What are they saying?"

Kitty turned to face her daughter in the back seat. "They are singing in an old language; it is an ancient song, which the slaves carried with them from Africa."

"Some sort of pocomania song," Mr. Savage added, a bit smugly, as if to contradict the tone of his wife's voice, which had a reverence, even a belief, to it. He parked his car by the roadside, so they wouldn't interfere with the procession, or the procession with them. He had no choice. The people were moving very slowly, and were in the middle of the road, treating the asphalt as if it were a forest track.

Soon the words of "Lead, Kindly Light, within the Encircling Gloom" reached them, and the voices of the people in the procession moved from the complexity of an African chant into the simplicity of an English hymn. "The night is dark and I am far from home"—these words sounded faintly as the line of mourners turned into a yard. Mr. Savage started the car again and the conversation became limited to Boy and Kitty and how long it would take them to reach town.

⁓

Kitty Freeman Savage was a very kind woman. If her daughter had to pick out a fault in her mother it would be her sense that Kitty held herself back from any contact which was intimate—with her daughters, friends, family. She seemed to save all her ability to touch for the man she was married to. Their arguments were violent, filled with the strength of the passion between them. Or so it seemed. Kitty complained that Boy was weak, and that he would never amount to anything; that he was intolerant of too many people; that he lived in another world. She complained that his presence in her life as her husband had essentially been an error—but she seemed to have no desire to change the situation. She made one attempt: one night when Boy came home incoherent from rum, with empty pockets, and the stench of sex about him, Kitty packed her things, grabbed her daughters, and phoned one of her brothers to come and get them. But the brother was away and Kitty could not drive; so she unpacked, and over the next weeks fought viciously with Boy, then forgave him.

The fighting between her parents frightened Clare. She did not think of their battles as violent—because she thought that violence meant someone had to strike a blow, and this they did not do. "I wouldn't hit you, Kitty, because I might kill you. Yes, I'd kill you for true," was what Boy sometimes said.

Clare had heard this statement from her father eight or nine times in her life that she remembered, during her parents' most unrelenting arguments, and the words chilled her, while at the same time becoming magical, a spoken amulet—if her father said this to her mother, she believed, then Kitty would remain unharmed. Clare was afraid that he would forget to say the words some wild evening, and then her mother would die. She tensed in her bed, listening to her parents' screams and shouts—the swearing of bitterness at one another—and couldn't sleep until Boy spoke as she hoped he would. "I won't kill your mother—not tonight." This was how Clare heard the words. There's nothing to be afraid of, she often told herself. Tomorrow they'll be having breakfast and going to work and kissing each other—they would never hurt each other. He would never hurt her. He loves her too much. People in love are just passionate—that's all.

But sometimes these assurances, made to herself softly under the light covers and behind the mosquito netting that made the space beyond her bed into a blur, did not work. Her mind sped: if he killed Kitty, then she would have to take responsibility, would have to call the police—become her mother and her father, the one dead, the other crumpled over his wife's body, raving, insane; at least, at the very least, roaring drunk and in tears. That was Clare's fantasy of what might be the final outcome of her parents' hostilities. She had seen it in the movies sent from Hollywood often enough. While at the very same time she told herself that such a thing was impossible. But her fears persisted, and she believed that her father could hold her mother's life in his hands. When the battle raged on and his words did not come to settle her, Clare tried to make herself sleep, trying to remember all the monarchs of England in consecutive order—trying to take her mind off the violence—but she said their fights were not violent. And she thought that her father, after all, was a good man.

With her children Kitty was restrained—in both anger and warmth. She didn't believe in too much physical affection between parents and children. It had not been her experience at all, and she never thought to change—if she actually ever thought about it.

While she saved all her physical and emotional passion for Boy, she saved most of her tenderness for people she barely knew. Kitty's daughters rarely saw her cry. If she did, it would be at a time like this, now as she watched the funeral procession of someone she had never known pass by, and she heard the voices of poor people remembering a song from Africa. She wept quietly in the front seat, hiding her tears from her family. The country people of Jamaica touched her in a deep place—these were her people, and she never questioned her devotion to them. She saved some of her paycheck from her job every week, and with the extra money she went downtown to buy dry goods, bags of rice, bottles of cooking oil, tins of kerosene, salted codfish, children's shoes, and other necessities, and got Boy to drive her to the country to find people to give these things to. She was not, and never considered herself, Lady Bountiful. She merely acted. She would not have swabbed the cut foot of an old man, or assisted at the birth of a baby, but she managed within her limits to "help people" as she called it.

Kitty had a sense of Jamaica that her husband would never have. She thought that there was no other country on earth as beautiful as hers, and sometimes would take Clare into the bush with her, where they would go barefoot, and hunt for mangoes or avocadoes out of season. Kitty believed that there were certain trees hidden in the underbrush which bore the fruit as they, the trees, wished—with no respect for ordained schedules, in a pattern not as God willed it. For her, God and Jesus were but representatives of Nature, which it only made sense was female, and the ruler of all—but this she never said.

Sometimes Kitty would take Clare to Annie's Hole, a small deep swimming place, where she washed her daughter's hair and the two bathed together in their swimming suits. It would never have occurred to Kitty to be naked with her daughter, and any intimacy between them abruptly stopped here. Clare told herself that it was enough that they were alone.

Kitty knew the uses of Madame Fate, a weed that could kill and that could cure. She knew about Sleep-and-Wake. Marjo Bitter. Dumb cane. Bissy, which was the antidote to the poison of dumb cane. Ramgoat-dash-along. She knew that you could kill someone with horsehair mixed with bamboo dust. She knew about Jessamy. About the Godwood: the tree of good and evil, which now hung behind the pulpit at John Knox in the form of a cross. She knew that if the bark of the tree came in contact with sweating pores, a human being would die quickly. She taught her daughter about Tung-Tung, Fallback, Lemongrass. About Dead-man-get-up. Man peyaba and Woman peyaba. About the Devilweed. She was convinced that the cure for cancer would be found in the bush of Jamaica—which could yield anything to she who would recognize such things. As a girl she had studied with the old women around and they had taught her songs like the one the funeral procession had sung. She was moved that such things had survived.

Around the countryside Clare saw women with big bellies pushing the waists of their dresses upwards, until the dresses caught under their armpits, and their spines curved inward from their burden. She never asked either one of her parents about these women. She knew what secret was kept safe behind the checked or flowered cotton, the bulge of flesh held in, it seemed, by the cloth. She saw other women sitting at the side of the road, with their babies in their arms, and their big wondrous breasts exposed to the sun. Brown skin pulled taut over their milk-filled breasts. Their babies sucked for all to see, their own eyes shut, and the women often closed their eyes as well, as the warmth of the sun and the sucking of their babies lulled them. She never asked her mother about this act. Somehow she was afraid it would hurt her mother to be asked. So Clare asked her father instead. "Something only animals do," was his brutal response. And she never knew if her mother had not done this with her because of Kitty's own way of being, or because she had applied Boy's sense of what was right— hardening what might have been a softness. Becoming less "animal" in the process.

"Cry-cry baby, suck your mama's titty," children used to taunt one another. At twelve Clare wanted to suck her mother's breasts again and again—to close her eyes in the sunlight and have Kitty close her eyes also and together they would enter some dream Clare imagined mothers and children shared.

"Yerry me a die, oh/Yerry me, oh/Country man a dig hole fe bury me, oh." Kitty sang softly under her breath as the two of them cut through the bush.

Chapter Eight

Kitty met Boy when she was nineteen and he was twenty-three, at a garden party on the grounds of the governor's residence, King's House, given for Jamaicans who had served His Majesty's victory in World War II.

Kitty's mother was both Black and white, and her father's origins were unknown—but both had brown skin and a wave to their hair. Her people were called "red" and they knew that this was what they were. No one had suggested to them that they try to hide it—were they able to. They were as old a family as the Savage family. All Jamaican families were old families. There had been no waves of immigration. No new settlers seeking a frontier. Only a settling of blood as some lighter skins crossed over one or other of the darker ones—keeping guard, though, over a base of darkness. And a trickle of white people, who worked in colonial offices, taught in private schools, supervised Bauxite excavations, bought retirement homes on the North Coast, or were regular guests at Round Hill Hotel—and who made the island seem whiter than it actually was.

The Freemans did not question this structure, or the fact that the white people brought money and seemed able to buy themselves any place on the island that suited them. The Freemans fit themselves into the structure and said that yes they were red people, and that was nothing to be ashamed of. At the same time preserving their redness.

These red people lived on a small farm. Mr. Freeman grew a few acres of sugar cane, and Mrs. Freeman kept a patch of yam, cassava, plantain, banana, okra, citrus; and there was wild ackee, guava, mango, tamarind, cashew, avocado. Martha Freeman, Miss Mattie, sewed the clothes for her six children, altering the discarded shirts of her elder sons for Kitty. Their house, where Miss Mattie would spend her entire life, was a frame house with four rooms: two bedrooms, a living room, and a dining room. Outside, behind the dining room, was a shed where they cooked; beyond that, the outhouse.

~~~~~~~

It was now August—a month of sudden storms but no sustained rain. Part of the time Clare spent with her grandmother. Clare sat in a corner of the kitchen, the shed behind the house, watching as the two boys, her cousin Ben and her half-cousin Joshua, squatted in another corner, talking softly together.

Outside the kitchen the air was warm and the sun was bright; inside the shed was dark and damp. Clare was sitting on the mahogany counter alongside the washed breakfast dishes. The counter was familiar to her. It had been worn and dented over time. Perpetual streams ran over its surface and gathered in small pools. Or they ran into the enamel dishpan which was set into the counter. It too was scarred, black shapes appearing where the white surface had been chipped away, looking like unmoving bugs—but only to someone who didn't know the dishpan. If you knew it, if you were accustomed to it day after day, you had memorized the terrain—the black shapes which became rivers, seas, and lakes. As you washed, the clarity of the map began to disappear. When the terrain was totally obscured by the film of Golden Guinea soap and hard cold grease, you knew it was time to change the water. When the black shapes threatened to change the whiteness into patches of water and themselves into land mass, then a new enamel pan was bought, and a new map created.

The only source of light in the shed was a window. A small space covered partly by a wooden shutter. Through the square of open space, Clare could see the backyard. The outhouse surrounded by a clump of pineapple bushes. The smoke from the open fire which clouded over the groups of men gathered in the yard. The avocado tree—now laden. The black hog hanging from the avocado tree, his snout almost brushing the earth.

Yesterday in that same tree she and Joshua had feasted secretly on the pears, the flesh mashed and spread across split halves of hard-dough bread, sprinkled with salt she had stolen from the "safe," her grandmother's screen-door cabinet which lived in the dining room, in which reposed spices and dry foodstuffs and Miss Mattie's communion wine. That same night they had played dominoes on the floor of the porch. Clare sitting crosslegged at a corner of the porch, Joshua standing on the ground, his chest reaching to where she sat. Their grandmother did not permit him to be where her granddaughter was. The two had slapped the dominoes on the painted concrete well into the night, until Miss Mattie called Clare inside.

Usually Clare would have feasted and played with her friend Zoe, but Zoe was away for a few days visiting her own grandmother at Lluidas Vale, so Miss Mattie allowed that Joshua could be Clare's playmate for the time being—until Zoe returned.

The hog hanging from the tree was dead, his throat slit by a small knife wielded by the boys' father. Clare had been ordered by Miss Mattie not to watch, so she had taken her place in the kitchen and watched only partly. Later, she was joined by the boys, who had watched up close, had even been part of it—holding the hog still for their father. They came into the kitchen filled with boasts and a claim that they appreciated the slaughter. Clare had not expected that the hog would scream, but he had, and his cries lacked any fierceness, only sounding fright across the yard, into the kitchen, through the house. Now, it was finished, and they were making plans about how to cut him apart. The open fire was going, fed by the dried stalks of coconut trees and brush collected from the last storm. Kerosene tins heavy with coarse salt were lined up outside in which the meat would be "corned." Some of the voices in the yard were raised, offering advice. Others were quiet, almost hushed in observance. Many in the groups only waited to see what the family would discard, and what they could get for their own tables.

The boys kept up their whispering, and occasionally laughed. Ben had taken time from school vacation to come down. Joshua did not go to school but worked for his grandmother full-time—he stayed on after his mother left for a better job in Kingston. His father had helped him to build a one-room house at the side of his grandmother's house. In it were a kerosene lamp, cot, dresser, and some old schoolbooks that had belonged to his father. And a square of open space through which daylight entered the room. Ben envied Joshua what he considered his freedom. They were both fourteen and Joshua had his own house and had done with school.

Joshua's skin was a deep brown, and Ben was almost as light-skinned as Clare, but the boys dressed alike: both wore khaki shorts and went barefoot and barechested. Both swam naked in the river together, while Clare was made to wear what they called a "bathsuit." She had hidden once behind a rock at the riverside and saw the two of them splashing each other's bodies—her eyes of course became fixed on their penises, and she compared these to her grandfather's swollen and purple organ, which in the clouds of his senility he had once shown her.

As she sat in the kitchen, she was aware of their conversation, but was unable to make out exactly what they were saying. Then Ben's voice came through to her.

"Go on, man, get de sint'ing fe me, nuh."

"Say pretty please."

"Okay, pretty please."

"But wunna mus' mek de fire."

"Good, man."

Joshua left the shed and went around the back. Clare watched him through the space in the window. He was asking a question. She saw his father, her uncle, her mother's brother, laugh and hand the boy his knife. Ben was busy building a fire with great concentration. When Joshua returned, he was smiling and laughing and carrying something wrapped in a leaf. There was blood on his khaki shorts but the knife in his hand was clean.

Ben spoke. "Good, man; give me de t'ing; mek me cook it."

Clare couldn't hold back any longer—it was as though she was invisible to the boys, who were acting like she wasn't there while knowing all the while she was. She knew that they would go on like this without once turning toward her; go on with their secret and their plans. So she asked them what they were cooking.

"Can't tell you," Joshua said, casually, without showing any surprise that she was sitting three feet away from him. He turned and smiled at her as he said it, the smoke from Ben's fire passing across his face. "Can't tell you."

"Can't I have some?" It had become so important to her to know what they were doing. What they were keeping from her. So important to be asked to join in.

"Dis sint'ing no fe gal dem."

"Why not?"

"Is jus' no fe gal pickney, dat's all." She had heard this before—spoken in different ways.

"Okay, I don't want none; jus' tell me what it is."

"No, gal. Wunna will tell Grandma. It no wunna business anyway. Is a man's t'ing." Ben had joined the conversation.

"No, I won't tell Grandma; I promise."

Ben turned to Joshua. "Well, brother, we not gwan get any peace unless we tell she." Joshua nodded and Ben explained to Clare. "Is de hog's sint'ing. His privates. Understand?"

She did understand. She looked away from the boys and looked down at the shapes in the dishpan, trying to fix her stare. Trying to concentrate on the white enamel and the spaces where it was gone. But the morning was coming back fast at her. And her inner eye recreated all the events of the hog-killing—in slow motion. The worst thing that could have happened to her, did. She hated to cry and she hated now that she couldn't control her tears—she was acting like a girl, in front of two boys who had just shut her out. She wanted more than anything to spill their fire and pour water over their delicacy and wreck their feast. She felt no sorrow now for the hog, whose penis and testicles were being roasted in a pan in her grandmother's kitchen. No sorrow for him a-tall, a-tall. She felt that keen pain that comes from exclusion. Out of control now, tears fell over her cheeks and her nose dripped. Her face changed—contorted and streaked. She screamed at them—"Piss on wunna! Piss on wunna!" They only turned back to their feast with a slight shrug, almost in unison, and she ran out of the kitchen and up the back stairs into the dining room.

She had to quiet her sobs. She did not want Miss Mattie coming out and asking her why she was crying. So she covered her face with her hands and tiptoed into the bedroom she shared with her grandmother. Through the wall, as she lay face-down on the doublebed, she could hear the voices of women. She could picture them in the parlor with her grandmother. Sitting in the bentwood rockers or on the dark brown velvet settee, which her grandfather had ordered from a catalogue one year when her mother was a girl and there had been a good cane crop. Now the rocker seats had been caned more than once, and the velvet had gone bald in prominent places, but these still were the seats of honor in her grandmother's house.

The hog-killing was a big occasion, an important social occasion, almost as festive as a wedding or a christening, or a Kingston garden party. And, as the men gathered in the backyard, smoking cigars made from jackass rope, and sipping from pints of Appleton Estate, their women and wives and daughters and sisters gathered to visit with Miss Mattie, to drink tea or soft drinks mixed into a cloudy punch with condensed milk, to chat in the house and on the porch and in the frontyard about the day and the past week and also speculate as to who might take home what part of the pig.

The bed was set against wooden louvers, and when she raised her head, Clare could glimpse the women on the porch and those standing around the guava tree in front. All were dressed in their best clothes, as she knew the women in the parlor would be. The space between the thin slats of the louver revealed a spectrum of dress which ran from navy blue to pastel to cotton printed with flowers and fruits and birds. Sleeved and sleeveless. High-neck and boat-neck and round-neck. Dresses which showed the symmetrical stitches of a treadle-powered Singer, or the tidy seams of chain stitches made by hand. Many of the dresses were decorated with embroidery or ornamented with appliqué. Both were art-forms of island women—things they learned so easily as girls, they almost did not need to learn them at all. Just give a country woman some thread and a needle and some cloth, and in a few hours she would have finished a woman's dress or a baby's bonnet or a man's shirt—decorated with initials or figures and made without a pattern. This art—the illumination of plain cloth with orchids and pineapples and hummingbirds—and this craft—the making of dresses and bonnets and shirts—had been passed through the lines of island women going way back. Far, far back—appliqué had been invented by the Fon of Dahomey, who had been among their ancestors.

Some of the women Clare could see wore hats—straw hats trimmed with shiny raffia wound into other images of flowers and fruits and birds, or perhaps an outline of the island, a ridgebacked elongated turtle, with the points of interest indicated by concentrations of color—Spanish Town a tight circle of red, Fern Gully a double line of dark green, Blue Hole a deep spiral of aquamarine. Some had turned their art to the making of these hats, which were sold to tourists in Kingston and Montego Bay in the crafts markets, along with the coconut husk banks and machetes etched with maps of the island on the blade.

Some of the women had straightened hair turned under into dark pageboys or pulled back into orderly buns. Others wore braids which they had strung with beads or ribbons. All the women were wearing shoes. Shiny dark leather oxfords, or low patent (pronounced with the accent on the last syllable) leather pumps. Most of the women in the yard wore sneakers—some without laces, some with the back smashed down, some with an opening cut to release a bunion, but all freshly whitened. In their hands they carried a purse, or a handker-chief knotted around their money.

The wrists of island women could tell the stories of their lives. Some clanked with silver bangles worn on both arms, their number in direct relation to each woman's status by way of her husband, common-law or church wedding, and her achievements by way of birthdays, anniversaries, babies born, children turned into successful daughters and sons. Like Miss Olive's daughter, Winsome, a geogra-phy teacher in a private school in Kingston, who sent her mama a sil-ver bangle on every conceivable occasion. The ears of the women also bespoke their standing, for the most part registered by the quality of the metal which hung from the holes in their lobes, drilled when they were babies. The women in the yard—that is, the poorer women—wore jewelry made from the red-eyed pods of seeds, dried in the sun and strung around their necks by themselves. Only a few of the yard women wore earrings (pronounced ears-ring); the ears of most had long since closed, had they ever been opened.

All the women spoke among themselves. But the groups were quite divided and few mingled. Those who did were making their way to the doorway to wish a "how you do" to Miss Mattie.

Now, concentrating on the parlor, Clare could hear her grand-mother's voice.

"Them tell me say Miss June is going to have de t'ing taken off."

"No. You don't tell me. What a terrible t'ing. A terrible fate."

"Yes, my dear."

The woman who responded to Miss Mattie was the retired school-teacher who lived across the road, Miss Naomi. Clare's grandmother was telling Miss Naomi about the cancer of the postmistress, who also ran the shop at the railway crossing. Clare thought she could guess what was to be taken off, since nothing had been named.

"Yes, my dear. The t'ing is the worst curse known to mankind. Is all around us. I tell you, Miss Naomi, if I didn't believe there was a god in heaven, I would be quite despairing. Quite despairing."

"Miss Mattie, it is the disease of our time."

Miss Naomi knew indeed what she was talking about. Two years earlier they had cut off her leg. But she still went back and forth, with a carved stick under her arm for balance, to the shop, to the Saturday market, to the river on Monday morning to wash. She no longer wore the *cotta* or carried the tin tub on her head. She had a niece, her late sister's child, to do that for her. The doctors had given her a new leg, as they called it, in Kingston, but she didn't trust it and it wasn't suited to the terrain, which was for the most part uneven and unpaved. Miss Naomi was Baptist, and only wore the leg on Sundays and Wednesdays to church, since the preacher had asked her as a favor to him. For herself, she was not shamed by her wound, but understood and accommodated the preacher's view that the sight of her might detract from the great glory of God, in whom all things were perfect.

"Poor Miss June," Miss Mattie said, "and her with neither a chick nor a child to take care of her."

Lying there in the bedroom, watching the women at this remove, Clare felt separated from them. Her mind was still back with what had happened in the kitchen. She should have kept her mouth shut. She should not have given the boys the satisfaction of knowing she felt left out—that they had the power to hurt her. Who would have wanted to eat that nastiness anyway. Why did they have the power to make her cry. But that was not the point. It was that last night she and Joshua had been friends and this morning he had gone so quickly, so easily, to the side of his half-brother. The car was at least a mile away and Joshua had taken off down the hill calling after Ben and racing to meet him. They had the power to hurt her because they were allowed to do so much she was not—she was supposed to be here, in this house, with all the dressed-up women.

She knew that if she opened the door and entered the parlor, she would have to spend the afternoon at her grandmother's side, greeting and speaking to all the visitors in the house, and answering their endless questions about school, her parents, life in Kingston. She was tall for her age, lanky, and as her father had noted, golden. Her wavy chestnut hair fell to her shoulders without any extraordinary means. On this island of Black and Brown, she had inherited her father's green eyes—which all agreed were her "finest feature." Visibly, she was the family's crowning achievement, combining the best of both sides, and favoring one rather than the other. Much comment was made about her prospects, and how blessed Miss Mattie was to get herself such a granddaughter.

She didn't want this. To have to answer questions and have her hair stroked while the women wondered at her. She wanted to leave.

Her grandmother thought she was out back with the boys; she could easily get away without being noticed—anyway her grandmother would be busy with her guests for hours more. Now that she was twelve, and "developing," Miss Mattie was more careful about her wandering about alone. She had instructed Clare never to go to the river by herself, nor to the shop. At the river Miss Mattie was afraid Clare would see the boys swimming naked; near the shop unemployed aimless men lounged with bottles of Red Stripe and might make remarks to her granddaughter, forgetting themselves. Clare could not go with the boys to hunt crayfish by the moonlight. Nor to build campfires behind the house at midnight to boil up yam and banana and fish. She could wander with Zoe—her friend whom she now missed—but she could not wander alone.

But she needed to wander alone right now. There was nothing for her here. She would never be able to tell these women what had happened in the kitchen, or explain to them how it made her feel. She let herself out the side door of the bedroom and went down to the darkness of the coffee piece.

Chapter Nine

Mad Hannah was in her usual place. Under the almond tree at a clearing at the end of the coffee piece and the beginning of the gully by the road. She was sitting there talking with a lizard.

"Massa Lizard, dem tell me say one duppy live inna dis tree. Tell Massa Duppy to show 'imself."

Mad Hannah saw Clare coming toward her.

"Afternoon, Miss Clare; how wunna do?"

"Not so bad, Miss Hannah; who wunna a 'talk to inna de tree?"

"Nuh one duppy what dwell here. You know dem say duppy have a liking fe de tree of de almond. No come no closer, or Massa Duppy will shine pon wunna and mek wunna head swell, or give wunna cramp, like what kill my poor boy Clinton, God rest him soul."

Clinton, the son of Mad Hannah, had been taken with a cramp while he was swimming in the river, and was drowned. People said that this had driven Mad Hannah over the brink, and turned her from being an *obeah*-woman into being a madwoman. Clinton was a big red man, who had returned from America about a year before his death, after having worked as a farm laborer. He was, as the saying goes, his mother's pride and joy, sent her back money and clothes and returned loaded with gifts. He moved in with her as soon as he got back from "Connect-ti-cut" and the tobacco fields there, and there was some comment that Clinton preferred the company of his mama to any other woman. There was a rumor around the place that he was being taunted by some of the other men and boys, and they had left him floundering in the water and gone about their business, while their shouts of "battyman, battyman" echoed off the rocks and across the water of the swimming hole. The swimming hole was now named for Clinton, because he had died in it.

Where they used to poke fun at Clinton, they now poked fun at his mama; who spent her days on "journeys" between almond trees— sitting underneath in her bleached flour-sack dress, head scarf made from some old rag she had collected. Her feet were thick and bare, the toenails hardened and yellowed like a hoof. She ate what she could beg from place to place, and sometimes slept underneath the trees which marked her journey. She went from tree to tree trying to raise the duppy of her son, to find the force which had left his body when he went under the water.

After his death, no one came forward to assist her in the rite of lay-ing the duppy at peace—no one came to chant that "the living have no right with the dead." There had been no arcade of palm, no white room with a white deathbed, no white rum or white fowl or white rice laid on banana leaves for the duppy to have his final feast—all was white because white was the color of death.

No one came to sing the duppy to rest and put bluing on the eye-lids of Clinton, nail his shirt cuffs and the heels of his socks to the boards of the casket. No one to create the pillow filled with dried gunga peas, Indian corn, coffee beans, or to sprinkle salt into the cof-fin and make a trail of salt from the house to the grave.

Before the slaves came to Jamaica, the old women and men be-lieved, before they had to eat salt during their sweated labor in the canefields, Africans could fly. They were the only people on this earth to whom God had given this power. Those who refused to become slaves and did not eat salt flew back to Africa; those who did these things, who were slaves and ate salt to replenish their sweat, had lost the power, because the salt made them heavy, weighted down. The salt sprinkled in the casket would keep the duppy in the ground, so he could not fly out, bring heat to the homes of the living, seizures to their children—he could not make their heads swell like a green coconut.

The night of the day that Clinton died, Mad Hannah carried him to their home on her back, laid his body on the bed, and rubbed lime and nutmeg around his nostrils and his mouth, under his arms and between his legs. She dressed him in his favorite clothes that he had carried from America. A red satin cowboy shirt and black lizard cowboy boots, blue-jeans, and a bright blue bandana around his neck. She went from yard to yard begging slats of wood, from crates, abandoned outhouses, in yards where inside plumbing had been installed, any bits and pieces she could find. That night she built his coffin and put him in it. The next day she traveled to the market and sold the clothes that he had bought her in Connect-ti-cut and paid two men to dig his grave in her yard. She bought two bottles of white rum, one for each of the men, and told them to be sure and pour a drink for the duppy before they took a drink themselves. But they ignored her, emptied the bottles into themselves, and fell into the grave, singing a song about a woman in Montego Bay. So Mad Hannah buried her son alone the next morning—when it should have been done at midnight.

On the third night after the burial she saw his duppy rise from the grave. She was sitting on her front step, between the strips of colored plastic which made a door, sipping some spirit weed tea, when she saw a mist rise in thin strands and gather over the surface of her son's grave. The mist became thick, turning from a gray fog into a white cloud, and drifted away from her, down the road, gathering speed and disappearing. She went into her house and marked the windowpanes with white crosses, and thought about how she had been made to fear her own son. Her gentle son who never did anyone harm. She knew that she had to find his duppy, to find it and work a spell with the two flat rocks she had gathered at the side of the river, and put him once and for all to rest. He must be somewhere.

⌒

"Miss Hannah," Clare asked, "is there any *obeah* in the privates of a hog?"

"Eh-eh, child, where wunna get such a t'ought?"

"De boys dem cut off de privates from de hog and roast dem and was gwan fe nam dem. Is magic?"

"De boys do all manner of sint'ing dem t'ink is magic. Dem not know a-tall, a-tall. Dem t'ink it gwan fe mek dem po-tent. To tek on de manhood of de hog."

"What is po-tent?"

"Means dem will have many many pickney."

"But dey only fourteen."

"Never mind, you hear, child. No bodder wid it. Boys t'ink 'bout dem t'ings more and more as de years go by. Mean no-t'ing a-tall, a-tall. Nice gal like wunna no fe bodder him head 'bout dis."

People made fun of Mad Hannah all around and all the time. They talked as she stood in front of them and they talked behind her back. They traced what they thought was her insanity. They mocked her dead son Clinton and said "him favor gal." They laughed at her journeys and her attempts to lay his soul to rest. And yet when they buried their dead they themselves took all the precautions she had been unable to take. They knew how Clinton had died and that his duppy might seek them out, so they put tobacco seeds over their doorways to keep him away, and made circles of coffee and salt around their yards to fend off his duppy. They chopped down any pawpaw trees near their homes, because duppies could taint the fruit of that particular tree and bring death. They did all these things, which in one way honored the spirit of the dead Clinton, and in another assuaged their guilt, but they couldn't bring themselves to speak kindly to his mother, or assist her in her quest.

These were men and women who had known Mad Hannah for donkey's years. They didn't stop to consider their actions. To ponder her relationship to magic. Or to think about her journeys as ceremonies of mourning, as expressions of her faith. They thought her foolish and crazy. Now she twitched where she used to stroll. She talked to lizards and spiders and turned away from many people on the road. They tried to forget that her actions followed on the death of her son. No . . . no, they said, she had passed through change-of-life too quickly and this had made her fool-fool. They extended their explanation: If she had not been fool-fool her son would not have been sissy-sissy. Because he was a sissy he was drowned. They forged a new chain of cause and effect by which her actions were bound. They removed themselves from any responsibility to Mad Hannah and her son Clinton—two people once in their midst.

They hounded Mad Hannah until one day not long after Clare had sought her out—one day when she decided she could take no more—she stripped off all her clothes and mounted the horse which Mas Charlie, the Baptist preacher, had tied to the shop railing, and she rode up into the hills to find some peace. Mas Charlie notified the police and they set out after Mad Hannah. It took them two or three days, but they found her by a stream asleep, the horse tied nearby. They sent her off to the asylum at Port Maria, where she tried to explain to the people in charge—the light-skinned educated people— about the death of her son and his incomplete and dangerous burial.

Chapter Ten

Christopher Columbus discovered—strange verb—discovered Jamaica in 1494, while on his second journey across the curve of the globe for Isabella and Ferdinand, los Reyes Católicos, the Catholic Monarchs. The series of his voyages began in 1492, the year he sighted Cuba and made a landfall on the island which became known as Hispaniola—later divided into the colonies of Haiti and Santo Domingo—the year the Jews were officially driven out of Spain, following centuries of persecution. Los Reyes Católicos are credited with unifying the Spanish realm on the Iberian peninsula, financing the discovery of America, enforcing the expulsion of the Jews, and soon after, the Moors, and initiating the slave trade between Africa and the Americas. In 1494 they negotiated the Treaty of Tordesillas, which divided the "non-Christian" world between Portugal and Spain: Portugal got India, Africa, and Brazil; Spain got everything else. The treaty followed a bull issued by Pope Alexander VI.

Christopher Columbus—whose statue stands in the town squares of so many countries of the New World—the Admiral of the Ocean Sea—the explorer whose body was buried four times: twice in the Americas, twice, and finally, in Spain—may well have been a Jew himself. At least some scholars are convinced of this. He came from

Genoa—perhaps entering Spain as a Marrano, that group of Sephardic Jews forced to hide their religion—and their identity—behind a pretense of Christian worship. There are Catholic churches in Spain with menorahs on their altars. His surname in Spanish was Colón; in Hebrew, Cohen. It is thought by some scholars that the logs aboard his flagship *Santa Maria* were kept in Hebrew. This man, whose journeys had such a profound effect on the history and imagination of the western world, is a relatively mysterious figure in the records of western civilization. He left behind him a reputation for dead reckoning—was he in search of a safe place for Jews—a place out of the Diaspora? So many veils to be lifted.

There was a Black man in Columbus's crew—Pedro Alonso Niño. And Black men sailed with Balboa, Ponce de Leon, Cortez, Pizarro, and Menendez. In 1538 Estevanico, a Black explorer, discovered Arizona and New Mexico. For what purposes did these men find themselves on their expeditions. So many intertwinings to be unraveled.

It was an afternoon in March—the month of most rain—the month in which the star apple ripens. Clare sat by herself in the Carib cinema—the first enclosed cinema in Jamaica, named for one of the native peoples of the West Indies.

The name of the Carib in their own language was *Galibi*. Carib was invented by Columbus, and was later changed to *Caníbal*—the origin of the English word *cannibal*—because it was said that the Galibi ate human flesh. The men of the Galibi spoke their own language; the women spoke only Arawak. They were a fierce warrior people who opposed the *conquistadores* with skill and power. The Galibi practiced scarification—the ritual marking of the skin. Their color was primarily cinnamon and their group later divided into Red Galibi and Black Galibi—the latter having mixed with West African peoples. The hair on their head was thick, straight, and very black; they removed all body hair ritually. They drank *paiwari*—a liquor brewed from the cassava plant.

They were all but exterminated by the Spanish conquerors. But they exist not only in the past—there are a few who survive today on a reserve on the island of Dominica.

The white inside of the cinema was interrupted by art deco carvings—flying fish, palm trees, doctor birds, pelicans—all came into relief in the shadows cast from the screen. Framing the screen were two elongated Galibi warriors.

Clare was cutting an afternoon of school—something she rarely did, and had never done alone before—because she needed to see this movie of *The Diary of Anne Frank*.

She knew *The Diary of Anne Frank*. She owned a paperback copy she had bought herself. It sat on the shelf over her bed, along with *The Last Days of Pompeii* and *Ivanhoe*, given to her by her father; the copy of *Treasure Island* she had won at prize-giving at school—in her white eyelet dress and black patent leather shoes she shook the hand of the woman mayor of Kingston, a dark woman, who said, "This is a wonderful book"; *Jane Eyre* and *Wuthering Heights*, favorites of her mother; *Great Expectations*; Delisser's *White Witch of Rose Hall*; and her great-grandfather's copy of Ovid's *Metamorphoses*, in which the gods transformed mortals into cattle, constellations, spiders, swans. Among this small collection was *The Diary of a Young Girl*, bent in at the spine, and partially hidden by the red leather of *Ivanhoe* and the brown cloth of *Treasure Island*. She was the daughter to whom books were given. Last Christmas, when her sister had gotten a pretend stove and a Tiny Tears doll, Clare was given a reading lamp and a desk. The two sides of the bedroom they shared reflected this difference between the two daughters: Jennie's babies, line up in a row, their blue-glass eyes fixed on Clare's bookshelf.

The cover of the paperback version of the diary was a photograph of Anne Frank, a small-seeming dark girl, with circles under her dark eyes, and a sweet smile on her face. Clare recognized the sweetness in that face, although she never named it as such, and often when reading the diary she would shut the book, her forefinger marking the place, to stare at the face of the writer of the diary and wonder about her and what if she had lived, had survived, and why did they kill her?

Why did they kill her? That was a question whose answer was always out of reach. It was hard for Clare to imagine someone, another girl, who was of her age or near to her age, dying—to imagine her dying as Anne Frank died, in a place called Bergen-Belsen, the year before Clare was born, was impossible. Last year, during the summer vacation at her grandmother's house, Clare had read in the *Gleaner* the announcement of the death of Claudia Lewis from leukemia. "Cancer of the blood," her grandmother had explained, the explanation casting even more strangeness on the death. How did her blood turn against her? Because that was what cancer did, Miss Mattie said, the body gradually poisoned itself.

Claudia had been a classmate of Clare at St. Catherine's. Someone she had barely known. And the pain in reading the obituary was not to be found, her anguish did not exist, in the fact that a friend or classmate had died, but in the realization which Clare now came to, that people of her own age—children—could die. None she knew had before.

At first, Clare tried to talk with her grandmother about all this—she asked for an explanation of her classmate's death at eleven. "No one is too young to die," was all Miss Mattie said, indicating to Clare by her tone that the decisions of her God were not to be questioned. It was a stern statement, and it would have been made kinder had Miss Mattie been able to tell her granddaughter about the death of her own youngest son from measles when he was thirteen. And whether that had shaken her faith any, or only served to make it stronger. But Clare was quieted by Miss Mattie's words and only watched as her senile and incontinent grandfather, a shadow-figure in this house, staggered across the porch and through the rooms, demanding to be fed, no one registering his presence until he became an annoyance, and she wondered why he wouldn't die, and why he wasn't dead already.

Her mind played a trick for her that summer, which made the death of another eleven-year-old girl easier to bear. The next day it began to seem to Clare that Claudia had not existed at all. This was simpler than thinking of her dying—that she should have come to an end. That this death was something for which Clare's own world should stop. When she returned to school after the summer, enough time had passed that Claudia's disappearance from this life was never mentioned by the other girls. And it was as though she had never been. And this trick took almost no effort at all.

But Anne most certainly had been here. She had left behind evidence of her life.

Clare knew that Anne Frank had been Jewish. And that *they*, the Germans, the Nazis, had killed her—one dark-eyed girl—for being

Jewish. Clare knew something of what had happened to the Jews of Europe under Hitler during the Second World War, the war her parents had been part of. The doctor who had delivered her had escaped from Germany himself. He stopped in Jamaica for five years waiting for a visa from America, and left to find the remainder of his family there.

When Clare asked her teachers to explain this fact of the history of the modern world, this overwhelming fact of the murder of six million Jewish people, the death of this one Jewish girl, the teachers hemmed and hawed. They talked about the London Blitz, the heroism of the British and the cowardice of the French, the character of Benito Mussolini, and the failure of the Weimar Republic and the Treaty of Versailles, which they said had brought on the war in the first place. Above all these words hovered the figure of Winston Churchill, whose speeches the girls had to memorize, in whom the teachers personified victory. "Sir Winston," they called him, a brilliant man who smoked cigars and drank brandy and slept in little silk undershirts. When Clare asked them—after listening respectfully to all their explanations and illustrations, and actually seeing their eyes fill up about the Battle of Britain—when she asked, "What about the Jews?" they sometimes talked about Jamaica as a haven for Jews suffering under the Spanish Inquisition. They sometimes mentioned the Jewish merchant class of Jamaica—"Who came here with nothing but a pushcart and some cloth, and *now* look at them." Which emphasis on the word *now* was never evident in their statements about the Chinese who kept most of the island's grocery stores or the East Indians who were dealers in silver and gold. But Clare was not yet able to detect this nuance in their speech and what it represented. Or the teachers mentioned the ancient synagogue at Crossroads, built by the Sephardic immigrants, and they described the cemetery where the Jews buried their dead.

When the teachers finally got around to the event known as the Holocaust, they became vague again—and their descriptions crystallized into one judgment: Jews were expected to suffer. To endure. It was a fate which had been meted out to them because of their recalcitrance in belief, their devotion to their own difference. This suffering was at once governed by the white Christian world, and when it seemed excessive, then it was tempered by the white Christian conscience. Unless, of course, it got out of hand and what her teachers called a "madman" came to power, and the "good" people didn't see that he had gone too far until it was too late.

The smoke from six million bodies burning had passed across the surfaces of continents and the slopes and peaks of mountain ranges and moved over bodies of water. The bones of six million people had been bleached stark white by the same sun that traveled overhead day after day, its circuits telling time. And when the bones started to crumble in their dryness, some of the dust had also been carried across land masses and bodies of water—while the rest seeped under the ground to fertilize the earth. The smoke from the bodies and the dust from the bones made a change in the atmosphere—in the air that people breathed and the water they drank. Did no one notice the steady change in their environment—that people were disappearing and returning as smoke and dust? Their lungs—their good Christian lungs—must have been filling with the smoke from burning Jewish bodies. Just as the clouds of Hiroshima and Nagasaki entered the bodies of women and emerged as milk from their breasts. A flash of light and then the imprint of a pedestrian who had vanished from a sidewalk in Hiroshima. The Jews vanished from cities and farms and universities and factories and shops and offices. It wasn't finished in a flash of light. It took years. How could they say they did not know until it was over. Until the Americans opened the barbed-wire gates and pledged the skeletons that this would never happen again.

But the teachers insisted: In the hot afternoon sun in a private girls' school built according to the principles of Victorian architecture— they insisted. No one in the world had any idea of what was going on in Germany—and the teachers always limited the swathe of the Holocaust to Germany—as if to isolate the enemy and fix the time when the barbarism of Attila overcame the rationalism of the Luther- ans. Out of all this came the crystallization that the Jews embraced suffering. They were born to it. The task of the white Christian was to see that his passion was not exploited—as it once—they said *once*— had been. The suffering of the Jews was similar, one teacher went on to say, to the primitive religiosity of Africans, which had brought Black people into slavery, she explained, but did not explain how she had reached this conclusion. That is, both types of people were flawed in irreversible ways. And though the teacher could have stopped at this, she went on to stress again the duty of white Christians as the "ordained" protectors of other peoples. And the class of Black, Brown, Asian, Jewish, Arab, and white girls listened in silence.

This twelve-year-old Christian mulatto girl, up to this point walk- ing through her life according to what she had been told—not knowing very much about herself or her past—for example, that her great-great-grandfather had once set fire to a hundred Africans; that her grandmother Miss Mattie was once a cane-cutter with a cloth bag of salt in her skirt pocket—this child became compelled by the life and death of Anne Frank. She was reaching, without knowing it, for an explanation of her own life.

When the teachers only confused her with their complicated statements, she turned to her father. One afternoon when she returned from school, after Dorothy had her "tidy," as all of a certain group of children were expected to, bathing with Yardley's lavender soap and changing into a red-and-white sleeveless Sea Island cotton dress and black patent leather shoes buckled across her instep and her crisp white socks, her hair plaited in two long braids which hung to her shoulders, bowed at their ends with red grosgrain ribbon—when she was thus "presentable," she walked onto the tiled verandah and sat beside her father on the mahogany and wicker settee and asked him about the Jews.

Boy began by running on and on that the Jews were smart people and should have known better than to antagonize Adolf Hitler, whom he characterized as a misguided genius in search of a scapegoat. When Clare pressed him for more information, he reverted to Christian dogma that the Jews had willfully, his word, turned their backs on salvation. She listened quietly and then asked him about *Ivanhoe*.

"But Daddy, in *Ivanhoe*, it is Rebecca who is the real heroine, not Rowena."

"Don't be silly, it's Rowena whom Ivanhoe chooses in the end; that's the point of the story."

"But it's obvious that he really loves Rebecca; isn't it?"

"Yes, he loves her, but Sir Walter Scott is showing that a Christian knight cannot be serious about his love for a Jew. She is an infidel in Ivanhoe's eyes. She is dark and Rowena is fair. Rowena is a lady—a Saxon. The purest-blooded people in the world. Rebecca is a tragic figure. You know that great writers often create their characters with tragic flaws, so that no matter what happens, they cannot succeed. They will never win in the end. Well, Rebecca's flaw is that she is Jewish—she is a beautiful flawed woman; and Ivanhoe is frustrated in his love for her. Of course she cannot help what she is."

"Why does Ivanhoe save her?"

"Because it is his duty as a Christian knight. But their love is doomed because they can never marry. They would be outcasts."

"What if I married a Jew?"

"Then you would be an outcast also." Mr. Savage said these words clearly and without raising his voice. He focused his eyes on the end of his cigarette where the ash was building up. Then flicked the cigarette toward the bank of yellow and gold bougainvillea which framed the verandah.

"But what if I loved him?"

"That does not matter one iota."

"Suppose he was only half-Jewish."

"It doesn't matter. A Jew is a Jew."

"Then how come you say I'm white?"

"What the hell has that got to do with anything? You're white because you're a Savage."

"But Mother is colored. Isn't she?"

"Yes."

"If she is colored and you are white, doesn't that make me colored?"

"No. You are my daughter. You're white."

Very simple. She pressed him again about the Jews.

"Do you think it was right to kill the Jews in the war?"

"Of course not."

"Then why didn't someone stop them? Why didn't all the ministers in the world stop them?"

"Well, we were trying to stop them, but it took time. And no one knew what was really happening. The Jews didn't even know. It was a terrible thing. But you know they brought it on themselves. They should have kept quiet. You can't antagonize someone like Hitler, you understand. The man was insane."

He had retreated back to that again.

"Daddy, suppose we had neighbors who were Jews; and Hitler came to power here. Would you turn them in, or keep quiet?"

"What a question!!"

"Well, would you?" Her legs were crossed at the ankles as she had been taught to do in school; it was the way "ladies" sat. She looked down at them, the brownness of her legs with their sparse golden hairs showing warm against the cool whiteness of her socks. Her knees tended to gray, and she had been given a piece of pumice—rough volcanic rock—by an aunt to work the gray out of her skin. She was waiting for her father's answer, but her mind was also back a ways and she was considering how she could be white with a colored mother, brown legs, and ashy knees.

Her father's answer finally came.

"Hitler could never come to power in Jamaica."

"But suppose he did. Or someone like him."

"There will never be another one like him."

"Well, let's pretend," something father and daughter often did together—let's pretend we are Aztecs; we are back two hundred years; we are explorers for gold. "Let's pretend, Daddy; what would you do?"

"Well, that would depend."

"On what?"

"On whether you and your sister and mother were in danger."

"Suppose we were all dead . . ."

"God, you are a morbid child!"

"No, suppose that Hitler had killed us for some reason, so you only had to worry about yourself. What would you do?"

"I don't know. You know, Clare, I sometimes feel that Jews were put on this earth only to put people like me in difficult positions. I mean, they are nothing but trouble sometimes—for themselves and for Christians. I wonder why God created them. Perhaps for that very reason. So they could test us."

All she now wanted was for her father to say that he wouldn't be a coward and that he would be brave. That was what she said to herself. She didn't think to ask him exactly who would meet the standards for him to extend his bravery—if he had any. Perhaps he had none—but she couldn't think that. And she was not aware that bravery was but a small part of it. A mass of confusion was in her mind. This was her *father* after all, she still held out hope.

"Daddy?"

"What is it now?" In the darkness of the verandah—because it had turned dark quickly that evening with only the briefest twilight—her father's presence was illuminated only by the shining end of his cigarette, a beacon which moved as he spoke to her. His voice was annoyed. She tried again.

"Do you think that God ordered that the Jews should die?"

"I don't know."

"Well suppose he did. If we are supposed to believe that everything God does is good—and that he does everything—then is it okay that they died?" She was struggling in her twelve-year-old mind, trying to meet her father across the ethics he professed.

"I didn't say that at all. I said I didn't know. I really don't know. There are more things in heaven and earth, Horatio . . ."

"Daddy, where is God?"

"You know that. God is everywhere. He is in space and in the heavens and the earth and the universe. He created all things and oversees all things. He moves in mysterious ways, his wonders to perform."

"But what is he like?"

"He is love. God is the source of all love. The force which has created all things in his image."

"Did he create the Jews in his image?"

"Yes."

"Then they are holy also?"

"Yes, of course; they are human beings, after all." After all . . . the two words sagged in the air.

"So why would God want them to die?"

"I never said he wanted them to die."

"But how could he let millions of people—millions of his children— die like that?"

"Enough . . . enough. I don't think you should try to understand something which is beyond your comprehension."

Chapter Eleven

In 1958 Clare began her study of the extermination of the Jews of Europe. She borrowed all the books available from the library on the subject; she forged her mother's signature and gained entry to the ADULT section. No one paid her much mind. There were very few books to be found in the small public library on the South Camp Road, but she borrowed them all, taking them home and hiding them under her mattress because she knew that her parents would not approve of her reading about these things. Her father had by now made his disapproval plain; and she knew too well of her mother's loyalty to her husband. She could hear her mother's response if she found the books: "Why do you want to bother your head with something that doesn't concern you; something so sad? You will only antagonize your father."

Clare read and re-read these books, trying to figure out *why* these events had happened. Not knowing that for her at this moment the why would be incomprehensible, always beyond reach, because to understand would be to judge her father capable of the acts which had formed and sustained the Holocaust. She was at that point at which some children find themselves, when to move forward would mean moving away. She was not ready or prepared for this action—perhaps later, if the place in her which might effect this was nurtured carefully, she could bring it off. Now—she felt only vaguely that she was doing something wrong. To find out why Anne Frank had died had become connected to a forbidden act.

To reckon with her father's culpability would also mean reckoning with her mother's silences—and to see how silence can become complicity. She felt *that* from time to time even now, but she didn't know it except as a danger specific to herself and she thought of it as part of a marriage. Something expected of a woman married to a man. As far as her daughters were concerned, Kitty Freeman Savage usually complied with her husband's judgment.

Clare then became a visualizer rather than an analyzer of the Holocaust. Placing these lives and deaths firmly in a past and place far removed from Jamaica—treating the event according to her father's word that such a thing would not happen here, and would never happen again. She found a book with the title *I Am Alive*, written by a survivor named Kitty Hart. And she tried to imagine Kitty's life in Auschwitz. The smokestacks and the barracks. The guards and the mud. The thousands upon thousands of women—because in Kitty Hart's book there seemed to be mostly women. Women who when they were able looked out for one another—this Clare held on to. She tried to piece Kitty Hart's day-to-day life together—as if anything in her own life had prepared her to imagine life in a death camp. She was a twelve-year-old light-skinned Jamaican—all she knew of the bounds of human misery were the alms houses she saw from the road and the shantytowns her father took great pains to avoid. And while she limited the Holocaust to Europe in her mind, her mind cast its environment in places that she knew on sight. Her mind tried to picture acre upon acre of shantytowns and acre upon acre of alms houses—and in this expanse of misery she placed inhabitants. Without thinking that these places were already inhabited with people the society had discarded, she filled her imagined camp with people like herself. People like her mother. People like Kitty Hart and Anne Frank. People, she told herself, who had no right to be there. In all of this she didn't really think of the people who were actually there. Had she done so, she would have probably concluded that they had done something which made their fates just. For that is what she had been taught. She was a colonized child, and she lived within certain parameters—which clouded her judgment.

She thought of the process by which clothing became ragged. Shoes wore out. She thought of hair being shorn. Bodies diminishing over time. She thought of the women's faces. Where they slept. The women taking each other's places in line. The orchestra of women which played during all of this. She tried not to think about the women who guarded other women.

Kitty Hart was about the age of Anne Frank when she was in the death camp. Clare wanted to know why one was able to live and one was forced to die. And she alternately imagined that she was each of them.

But she was a lucky girl—everyone said so—she was light-skinned. And she was alive. She lived in a world where the worst thing to be— especially if you were a girl—was to be dark. The only thing worse than that was to be dead. She knew the composition of her school and the constraints of color within. An unease seemed to live in a tiny space in her soul—for want of a better word—and she was struck by what she told herself was unfairness and cruelty while at the same time she was glad of the way she looked and she profited by her hair and skin.

Clare had learned that just as Jews were expected to suffer in a Christian world, so were dark people expected to suffer in a white one. She remembered an incident when an old Black woman was standing at the bus stop across from school and approached two of Clare's classmates and asked them the time. The old lady was dark-skinned and shabby-looking. And the classmates were darker than Clare was— one girl was a scholarship student, the other was the daughter of a civil servant. When the old woman asked the girls to tell her what time it was, they turned away from her and told her to mind her own business. Clare watched this and went over to the old lady, gave her the time, and the threepence busfare she begged, and turned to hiss a question at her classmates: "How could you be so inhuman?"

She decided then and there never again to speak to these girls. She did not tell anyone about the incident and she didn't really know why it happened or why the word "inhuman" was the word which came so swiftly into her mind. Clare did not understand enough about her world and her place in it to question why the old lady had approached the other girls and not herself. Nor could she begin to understand why the two dark girls had responded as they had. That old lady, in her ragged clothes and mashed-down shoes, was only a sad person—a sufferer—to her. Clare could not be expected to identify with the old lady or her darkness, her poverty or her position of sufferer. She did not think that it was different for her classmates—that they hoped to pass or were being trained to pass beyond the suffering and the expectation of their oneness with this state of being and to make a separation for themselves. "A better life."

Again—she did not analyze; she observed. And after that she made her judgment.

"Inhuman" was a horrible word to call anyone. It could mean that you were behaving in an "uncivilized" way. That you were being cruel beyond the bounds of expected human cruelty. Or that you were a "dirty dog," and therefore not human at all. The question of humanness or the lack of it had been purified in the crucible responsible for the society in which this girl now found herself. The society had been built around an absolute definition of who was human and who was not. It really was that simple—except some people were not quite one thing or the other.

When clarity diminished, one thing remained. The sufferer was not expected to be human. The sufferer would not give himself or herself over to suffering were he or she human. Human suffering was the fault of no one but the sufferer. The sufferers were responsible for their own miserable lives. The Arawaks—who had named Jamaica, Xaymaca, land of springs—existed no longer. One old book written by a Dominican missionary said that the Spanish had fed the Arawaks to their dogs because they found them less than human. The name Arawak meant "eaters of meal," a reference to cassava—the staple of their diet.

When he left on his journeys across the curve of the globe, Columbus carried with him several books in which the white Christian European imagination had carved images of the beings in unknown and unexplored lands. Dog-headed beings with human torsos. Winged people who could not fly. Beings with one foot growing out of the tops of their heads, their only living function to create shade for themselves in the hot tropical sun. People who ate human flesh. All monsters. All inhuman. The people the explorers and the philosophers of exploration envisioned would inhabit the ends of the earth.

In part the Europeans created these fantastic images to render the actual inhabitants harmless. Like putting a face on God to minimize the terror. They were not unlike modern-day science fiction writers— those who create alien hordes who spill their own green blood on the spinning asteroids where their extraterrestrial battles are fought. The true inhabitants will always be less fearsome than these imaginary creatures and therefore easier to conquer.

Imagined inhabitants will have few—if any—individual characteristics. They will have bizarre features by which they are joined to one another, but none which are specific to themselves. Their primary feature is their difference from white and Christian Europeans. It is *that* heart of darkness which has imagined them less than human. Which has limited their movement. The fantasies of this heart infected the Native tribes of North America with smallpox and with syphilis. Destroyed the language of the Mayans and the Incas. Brought Africans in chains to the New World and worked them to death. Killed nine million people, including six million Jews, in the death camps of Europe. This is one connection. These are but a few of the heart's excesses.

Clare had called her classmates "inhuman"—and it would take her years to recognize the source of this word—to understand that while their act toward the old woman was a sad act, it had a foundation.

Now, in the cinema, the actors in the movie talked out of the diary, but Clare knew enough of the book, or had her own by-now-deep ideas about it, that not all of the movie rang true to her. The actress playing Anne was all wrong: she was too pretty, too healthy-looking, did not show any outward effect of living in a crowded attic, in a cramped space with no privacy and little nourishment. What did ring true—and what had in the diary—was the relationship between Anne and her mother.

It may well have been that this relationship touched Clare in such a way that her interest in the *why* of the Holocaust originated. The relationship was mostly influenced, it seemed to Clare, by the remoteness of Anne's mother. She was a woman held back. Restrained by what seemed a combination of dignity and sadness. The connection which held Clare's interest in Anne Frank and her death began with her own mother and moved outward, to a sympathy with Anne.

Would Anne have lived to see her liberation if her mother had been different? Would Anne's mother have been different if the Holocaust had not happened? Where *was* the source of her coldness? Where did her remoteness come from? The mother of Kitty Hart, about whom they had not made a movie, stood in contrast to the mother of Anne Frank. She had fought for her daughter's survival. She had stolen food from the dead for her. She had hidden her when she was sick, so her daughter wouldn't be selected for death. Did Kitty survive because her mother had confronted the horror and taught her daughter to live through the days?

Anne's mother died. Then Anne's sister died. Then Anne died.

Those mornings and afternoons with her mother in the bush sometimes made Clare think—wish—that they were on a desert island together—away from her father and his theories and whiteness and her sister and her needs. That they would survive on this island with just the fallen fruit her mother gathered. And she wanted this.

The movie finished when the green police came for the Franks and the other people in hiding. The lights in the Carib came on, Clare dried her eyes, and was soon on the street at Crossroads walking towards the Woolworth's. There she bought herself a diary—pink-plastic-covered, illustrated with the caricature of a teenaged girl on the cover, an elongated figure with a pen in her hand. The only diary available, it came with a lock and key. Clare paid her five shillings, locked the empty book, and put the key in her pocket.

She took it home and wrote about the movie and about Anne. She looked again at the beautiful face on the paperback cover and tried to imagine her at the end. Did another woman hold her, or did she die by herself?

Kitty—the name of Clare's mother and one of her heroines—was the name that Anne Frank had given her diary. As if in that attic hiding-place she was writing to a friend. One in whom she had complete trust—she wrote that. Clare did not tell her mother anything which was close to her. She avoided any subject which she thought would make her mother uncomfortable. She did not tell her when she found the powdered rubber disk on her mother's bureau—she did not ask what it was. She assumed that it was private—things made of rubber usually were. Like the hot water bottle and curved tube hanging from the back of her aunt and uncle's bathroom door. These things only made her mother speechless and sometimes angry. "You'll know soon enough."

So she could not take the name Kitty for her diary—she did not know what to call it.

Chapter Twelve

When the wispy hairs began to grow between Clare's legs and under her arms—slowly, slowly—it was only Zoe she told, only Zoe she showed them to. And Zoe showed her own hairs. Quick glimpses. And then giggles as the parts were covered over.

Clare considered Zoe her closest friend. She lived in the country-side, in St. Elizabeth, near to Clare's grandmother. Of the six acres Miss Mattie owned, she saved one on Breezy Hill; piece by piece she loaned it to people in need of some ground to live on. Zoe lived there with her mother and sister, in a wattle house with a palm-thatched roof, and pages of the *Gleaner* pasted across the inside walls. The out-side walls were bright with whitewash. There were two beds in the one-room house: a double iron bedstead, where Zoe and her mother slept, and a small cot for her younger sister.

Miss Ruthie made her living by going to the market at Black River every Saturday and selling some of the crops she raised on the quarter-acre she borrowed from Miss Mattie, and the pink-edged coconut cakes and dark brown tamarind balls she made on Friday night. Sometimes she and her daughters gathered cashews from the two trees near the house, blanched and roasted them, and added them to the long deep basket she carried with her. Mostly she sold callaloo, tomatoes, oranges, mangoes, yam, and cassava. She left Saturday at daybreak, traveling the distance on an old open-back truck which belonged to Mas Fred-die. He had painted it a bright green and deep purple and had printed the word LIGHTNING on the driver's cab door. Mas Freddie filled the back of his truck with fifteen or twenty marketwomen, each pay-ing him a shilling, each loaded down with her basket, trying to pro-tect her fruit and tomatoes from bruises as the truck bumped and banged along the country road and the women crowded each other on the long slatted seats.

On the way to Black River they passed the dirt road to Accom-pong Town, the oldest settlement of freedmen and freedwomen in the western hemisphere, and all turned their heads to try and catch a glimpse of the mysterious Maroons—about whom they knew little. It was said that the women of the Maroons all had straight black hair and that they still dressed as they had in Africa.

The women gossiped and talked on their way to the concrete square in Black River, where they spread their blankets and mats, and arranged their fruits and vegetables and other things to sell, and squatted or sat, speaking out to the people walking by, telling them that their goods were the freshest and not to be passed up.

"Why wunna look pon him goods, missis? Wunna no say him goods is las' week sint'ing?"

"Come here so and see fe me ackee, fresh-fresh, pick dis mornin'."

"Beg you jus' tes' me mango—is fine fine."

Black River was a small market town; there were no tourists ambling about, paying the marketwomen sixpence to pose for a photograph—more if they agreed to show their gap-toothed smiles. No *buckra* people were here at all—just country people, country women mostly, not unlike the market women themselves, just looking to buy one *sint'ing* for their families which they themselves did not raise. It was a hard life—selling things to people as poor as they were—and, by the late evening, on the way back to their yards with Mas Freddie, the women only had earned a few shillings to get them through to the next weekend. Their baskets might be half-empty, but this was because they had given away some of their goods to women who asked them for a little something, and it felt better to do this than to carry the almost-laden baskets back home.

In those days the calypso was at its height of popularity, and Harry Belafonte, himself a Jamaican, was singing on American television and in American nightclubs of the "island in the sun" and the "pretty gal" he left back in Kingston town. One song was arranged in calypso tempo, all smiling children and ever-bearing trees. It was a lament, a traditional song of marketwomen; sometimes, on the back of Mas Freddie's truck in the cool of a late Saturday night, passing by the roads which led into the territory of the Maroons, the marketwomen sang—

> *Carry me ackee go a Linstead Market*
> *Not a quatty-wuth sell*
> *Carry me ackee go a Linstead Market*
> *Not a quatty-wuth sell.*

Lord, what a night, not a bite
What a Satiday night
Lord, what a night, not a bite
What a Satiday night.

Everybody come a feel up, feel up
Not a quatty-wuth sell
Everybody come a feel up, feel up
Not a quatty-wuth sell.

Lord, what a night, not a bite
What a Satiday night
Lord, what a night, not a bite
What a Satiday night.

All de pickney dem a linga, linga
Fe wah dem mumma no bring
All de pickney dem a linga, linga
Fe wah dem mumma no bring.

Lord, what a night, what a night
What a Satiday night.

⁓

Zoe was Clare's age, and went to the school which had been Kitty Freeman's school—held in a cement-block back room which had been added on to an old stone church. The school, which consisted of one class, was led by Mr. Lewis Powell, a tall and *mauger* yellow man, who had instructed all the children around and about, from six to fifteen years old, in the same small hot room, for twenty-five years.

Mr. Powell *preffered* the title schoolmaster to teacher, and he ran his school along similarly old-fashioned lines. He had a temper when his discipline was crossed, and the children were accustomed to having their knuckles cracked by his bamboo switch. For talking out of turn, misremembering a given assignment, making a nuisance in the classroom, and, in the case of some of the younger children, for "not holding your water." But the few strokes of the bamboo switch—

applied lightly, because Mr. Powell felt sympathy for these little ones—was not as bad as being led from the classroom by one of the older girls, to be washed and rinsed and set in the sun to dry.

The room had chairs and two long tables, around which the children sat. There was no blackboard, but each student had a square piece of slate and a stick of white chalk with which they recorded almost every word that Mr. Powell said, and did their sums and exercises.

Zoe walked to school barefoot every morning, a distance of about a mile, her white sneakers hanging around her neck by their laces, to save their soles. She was as tall as Clare, and darker; her hair wound in braids around her head. She wore a blue tunic made of heavy cotton and a light white Sea Island cotton blouse underneath—one given her by Clare, who had gotten some new ones when St. Catherine's changed their style from breakneck to Peter Pan. The collar of the blouse was "crisply creased," as Mr. Powell demanded. Every evening when she came home, Zoe rinsed her blouse and spread it on a bush to bleach and dry, then heated a flatiron over some coals and stroked the cotton until there were no wrinkles and the collar line was sharp. Her uniform—blue tunic and white blouse—was the one adopted for girls who attended the state schools in Jamaica; the uniform for boys consisted of khaki shirt and shorts, bleached stainless, starched, and pressed every morning before school—"There should be a knife-edge from your waist to your knees," Mr. Powell told the boys. He did not mind patches, as long as the patches could not be easily noticed.

Mr. Powell's teaching manuals were forwarded to him by the governor's office, which in turn had received them from a department of the colonial office in London—that department in charge of organizing the state education of the children in the crown colonies. These manuals, for the most part, stressed reading and writing and simple arithmetic. The history, of course, of the English monarchs. The history of Jamaica as it pertained to England—the names of the admirals who secured the island from the Spanish, the treaties which had made the island officially British, the hurricanes and earthquakes which had stirred its terrain and caused the failure of cash crops, the introduction of rubber planting after sugar failed, the importation of "coolie" labor after the slaves were freed—all these things were dated and briefly described, and the class competed to see who had memorized them most perfectly.

The manuals also contained instructions for teaching literature: Mr. Powell was told to have the younger children read poems by Tennyson, the older ones, poems by Keats—"supplied herewith." To see that all in the school memorized the "Daffodils" poem of William Wordsworth, "spoken with as little accent as possible; here as elsewhere, the use of pidgin is to be severely discouraged." The manual also contained a pullout drawing of a daffodil, which the pupils were "encouraged to examine" as they recited the verse.

Mr. Powell received the exact same manuals year after year. For twenty-five years he had been told in the same words and by the same methods what he was expected to impart to his students. The manuals took notice of the fact that the ages of the children varied, but not that the identity of most of the children did not change over several years. Mr. Powell wrote to the governor's office that with all due respect the colonial office seemed to think that each year would bring an entirely new class to his cement-block room in St. Elizabeth, which was of course not so—and would the governor please look into this matter. Yours faithfully, etc. But no reply ever came.

The manuals were oblivious to any specific facts about the nature of Mr. Powell's class. No doubt the same manuals were shipped to villages in Nigeria, schools in Hong Kong, even settlements in the Northwest Territory—anywhere that the "sun never set," with the only differences occurring in the pages which described the history of the colony in question as it pertained to England.

Probably there were a million children who could recite "Daffodils," and a million who had never actually seen the flower, only the drawing, and so did not know why the poet had been stunned.

Mr. Powell was a lover of poetry. In his room provided for him by the parish council, behind the largest grocery store in the vicinity, he wrote poems about all manner of things. He decorated the walls of the room with his poems, printing them in black ink with his quill pen on the backs of the daffodil drawings he had been sent over the years. So when he lay on his bed, his own words were visible to him.

As a young man, in the 1920's, Lewis Powell had traveled to New York City. There he pirouetted around the edges of the Black literary movement known as the Harlem Renaissance. He took with him a letter of introduction to the Jamaican poet Claude McKay, and Claude brought him along to meet other Black poets, novelists, editors. The Black nationalist Wilfred A. Domingo, another Jamaican, took a poem of Mr. Powell's and printed it in his paper *The Emancipator*. Partly because the poem was a good poem—a short verse description of traveling to America on a United Fruit boat, carrying bananas from Port Antonio to Miami, "working as a hand among hands"—partly because Domingo wanted to help his young compatriot along.

British West Indians, as most island people were called, had to stick together in Harlem, even among the intellectuals involved in Renaissance and Nationalist circles. It seemed sometimes that Black Americans didn't really trust Black West Indians—all were of course of African descent, but each group had been colonized differently. The differences between them ranged from food to music to style to their way of being in the world. Lewis heard his people called all manner of things—the Americans said that the West Indians were too uppity and didn't know their place. They called them Black Jews— half in admiration, Lewis felt, half in scorn. Because West Indians in Harlem—that is, the ones who had managed to make the journey to Harlem, settle their families, find work—saw themselves as business people, favored private enterprise, bought property with the earnings they salted away, and were determined to steer their children to the professions. This became their image. The Americans said the West Indians were too intent on status. Too concerned with achievement. All this irked some of the Black Americans the West Indians lived among—after all, the "monkey-chasers," as the West Indians were called by their neighbors, were outsiders, people from tiny little islands who did not belong in Black America.

Even worse than their ways with money and property, the Americans thought, was the imitation by Black people from Jamaica, Barbados, Grenada, Trinidad, Tobago, and so on, of the things the English brought to the islands, which the West Indians now brought to Harlem. These were people who played cricket on weekends. Who held balls in honor of English monarchs, English holidays. Who flew the Union Jack over their shops and real estate offices. Who seemed to think they were something they were not.

During his time in Harlem, Mr. Powell became acquainted with one of the women writers of the Renaissance, whom he met one afternoon at one of A'lelia Walker's salon gatherings. This Zora struck him immediately as a beautiful and strong-willed woman. Talk about "uppity"—Lord have mercy. No island woman would dare to do the things Zora took it upon herself to do. No island woman would travel into the Haitian bush alone to study *vodun* when everyone knew that Haiti was just crawling with zombies and snakes and all manner of badness. And her jokes—some raw laughs they had with Zora. But Zora had style—and the woman could write like a dream, Mr. Powell thought. Even now, in the green depths of St. Elizabeth thirty years later, he remembered her smile and her talk and wondered if she was still alive. She must be, and she must be going strong.

When she came to Jamaica in the thirties to do the fieldwork for her book *Tell My Horse*, Mr. Powell insisted on accompanying her on some of her journeys into the Maroon settlements of the Cockpit Country. But Mr. Powell had not liked her book a-tall, a-tall. Just like Zora to pretend that Jamaicans were comical and uncivilized—little better than Pygmies in the jungle; at least that is what Mr. Powell felt. Zora accentuated the African customs too much, what remained of them, far too much; those things that had left so many of the country people he knew superstitious. And led them into all manner of foolishness. This was not the way Jamaica should take—these barbarian things should be made as little of as possible. Superstition was fine in poetry or stories, Mr. Powell contended, but not in practice. This superstition, and the "ignorance" which accompanied it, was too prevalent in Jamaica—and Mr. Powell blamed it absolutely for the death of his friend Clinton. And that old mother of his, the one they came and finally took to where she belonged, nothing but a damned witch. She was to blame as well. These people—whom he never forgot as his people—had to be taught to rise above their past and to forget about all the nonsense of *obeah* or they would never amount to anything.

After Wilfred A. Domingo accepted his poem, Mr. Powell came by his offices now and then to talk about Black nationalism and what Black people should do to raise themselves to the level of whites and eventually surpass them. Domingo was a serious political thinker, one who had joined with A. Philip Randolph and others during the First World War to argue for a Black boycott of the American armed services. Why should Black people die for America in Europe, they argued, when they were already dying for America in America? America had lynched and raped and burned their bodies in the country they had lived in for hundreds of years—the country they had built themselves. It was a simple and powerful argument but it did not stop thousands of Black men from enlisting in Black regiments and proving their courage and loyalty to what was said to be the American way of life in overseas combat, where many of them were killed. Just as many were killed at the same time in the various groves and forests of the United States. Morally, Mr. Powell reasoned, Black people may have already surpassed white people—but they needed to show their superiority where it counted for something. And his association with Domingo and others led him to another radical, one who trucked with no half-measures and believed profoundly in the future of the Black race—Marcus Garvey.

Lewis Powell joined Garvey's Universal Negro Improvement Association, which was based on the Jamaica Improvement Association Garvey had founded in his homeland. Garvey's dream of the Black return to Africa became Mr. Powell's. But it would not be a bushman's Africa—it would be an aristocratic and civilized Black continent, where, finally, after hundreds of years of misery, Black supremacy would be evident, and Black people would prove once and for all that they were capable of existing in a white-dominated world on their own terms.

An enormous red plume was what first came to his mind when Lewis Powell recollected Marcus Garvey—Provisional President of Africa. An enormous red plume curling skyward from Garvey's old-fashioned military-style hat. A small dark man with a huge head and tiny beadlike eyes, Garvey received his followers from a velvet chair, his incongruously long and elegant hands gesticulating, and the red plume trembling as he spoke of Africa, the land of opportunity for Black people—the only place on earth which would support their freedom. Home.

Garvey's plan seemed perfectly logical to Mr. Powell. And with his vociferous passion and the light that jumped from his black eyes, Marcus convinced many more. This was the way of the Black future. He gave his people parades—filled with marching bands, the African Motor Corps, African Legion, Black Star Nurses—all but the nurses dressed in Black and Green and Red and Blue. People and Land and Fire and Sky. People and Jungle and Blood and Sea. He bestowed titles on some of his adherents—duke of the Niger, countess of the Gold Coast, knight commander of the order of Ethiopia. Placing an English construct over his dream of Africa—for this, people made game of him. As if a Black lord or lady was a comical thing. This was the twenties, when the prince of Wales danced at the Cotton Club. Some poked fun, others thought him a romantic. Jesus and God and the Virgin Mary were Black—Satan and Beelzebub and Lucifer were white. But Mr. Powell knew the one truth about Marcus Garvey—his love of Black people was unshakeable and his belief in the beauty of things Black was uncompromised. He wanted the best for his people. The best as he saw it. The best as he had taught himself it would be.

It was not meant to be. It had not been meant to be. That is what Lewis Powell thought now as he looked at the framed stock certificate hanging over his writing table. The Black Star Shipping Line. Five shares at five dollars a share. For that and other things Garvey had been arrested and put in jail in the American South. In Atlanta. A federal penitentiary. A small dark man with his immense dream had been watched over by the narrowest of minds in a holding pen—a *barracoon*—for two years. Then they shipped him to Jamaica. And in 1940 he died in London: a burned-out and broken-hearted man who with his thousands of followers might have been the difference.

With Garvey, Mr. Powell found an excitement he never found again.

There was a lot of class time to be filled in Mr. Powell's school. Time left open by the repetitions of the manuals, which he only briefly described and then discarded. So Mr. Powell taught his class to recite poetry and he told them the lives of the poets as well as the poems themselves. He spoke to them about Black poets as well as white ones. Langston Hughes collided with Lord Tennyson. Countee Cullen with John Keats. Jean Toomer with Samuel Taylor Coleridge. He read McKay alongside Wordsworth.

> If we must die, let it not be like hogs
> Hunted and penned in some inglorious spot,
> While round us bark the mad and hungry dogs,
> Making their mock at our accursed lot.
> If we must die, O let us nobly die,
> So that our precious blood may not be shed
> In vain; then even the monsters we defy
> Shall be constrained to honor us though dead.

He gave his students these words—and the children copied them out on their slates and spoke the poem back to him. He told them it was a poem about dignity, about people becoming better than they thought they ever could. Realizing that they too were precious. But Mr. Powell stopped there—keeping the context of the poem—the reason of the poem—to himself. The Red Summer of 1919. The summer which was red because of the blood which was spilled across the United States. Twenty-six race riots. Washington. Chicago. Omaha. Knoxville. Other places. Black people fought back. Violently. With guns. And they killed white people as they themselves were killed.

Better the children should not know this part of the history—America was America anyway, and not for West Indians. At least, not for those who could not pass. Garvey had been destroyed there. Another Jamaican who should have stayed home. These children lived in a country which kept them poor and wanted to keep them ignorant, but at least it didn't lynch them, didn't put them in jail for no reason, Mr. Powell told himself. At least they could travel freely—if they had the means. Education. Education in the finer things of life was better than education which would only lead the children to sadness and discontent. So he gave them McKay's poetry and Hughes's poetry and Toomer's poetry because he wanted them to know that there had been songs by Black men which were equal to any songs by Englishmen. But he concealed the sources of many of the songs and the lives he told them about the poets became the lives themselves.

He had them recite "The Negro Speaks of Rivers" and transform the rivers named by Langston Hughes into the rivers of Jamaica—these were the rivers which would make their souls grow deep. These were the rivers they knew and should know. They had no business with Mississippi or Congo or Nile or Euphrates. Better to be content with Black. Plantain Garden. Salt. Yallahs. Cobre. Minho. Martha Brae. Great Spanish. White. The history of Jamaica was held in these waters. And so were the lives of these children.

During the final week before the annual three-month summer break, Mr. Powell organized what was known as his Jamaican Tableau, in which all the children took part. The sanctuary of the church was decorated with palm fronds, the altar dressed with fruit, and the children were made to represent mountains, flowers, birds, and rivers.

All families who were able came to the performance, and filled the seats to watch their children act out Mr. Powell's visions. He had chosen Zoe for the final event of the program, the recitation of one of Mr. Powell's favorite poems. She stood in the pulpit, dressed in her best dress, with ribbons braided through her hair—

> *"Maroon Girl, by Walter Adolphe Roberts*
>
> *I see her on a lonely forest track*
>   *Her level brows made salient by the sheen*
>   *Of flesh the hue of cinnamon. The clean*
> *Blood of the hunted, vanished Arawak*
> *Flows in her veins with blood of white and black.*
>   *Maternal, noble-breasted is her mien;*
>   *She is a peasant, yet she is a queen.*
> *She is Jamaica poised against attack.*
>
> *Her woods are hung with orchids; the still flame*
>   *Of red hibiscus lights her path, and starred*
>   *With orange and coffee blossoms in her yard.*
> *Fabulous, pitted mountains close the frame.*
>   *She stands on ground for which her fathers died;*
>   *Figure of savage beauty, figure of pride."*

Mothers and grandmothers, sisters and brothers, aunts and uncles, and fathers and grandfathers—all were silent as Zoe recited. They were taken by the poem. They could recognize the poet's images and his words. They knew hibiscus, mountains, forests, orchids. They knew of the legend of the Arawak—sometime ago a young brown man had come to their area to dig for relics left by the Indians. The Arawaks had been pure and peaceful; there were no weapons to be found among their leavings. These people had also heard of the Maroons—but like the people in the Tabernacle in Kingston, the people in this country church did not know of the wars the Maroons fought. Their minds now cast separate images of the Maroon Girl in the poem. They saw her naked or clothed, quiet or fierce—they saw her cinnamon, as

the poet wrote; or imagined her skin the nutmeg color of Zoe, who
had read the poem with "great seriousness" and "great nobility," as
Mr. Powell had coached her.

After the reading, the people dispersed and the children left for
their vacation.

Chapter Thirteen

Zoe and Clare met one August when each was ten, and Clare had
no one to play with. Miss Mattie did not want her to disturb
Joshua at his work, getting in the way as he carried water from the
river and forever bothering him to play catch or tag or dominoes when
he was supposed to be feeding the hogs. And she was getting too old
to be running around with boys anyway. But there was not much to do
in the country alone. Without someone to join with, the days stretched
out and the only way to fill them was to read—schoolbooks or newspapers or the Bible—or to walk within the limits set by Miss Mattie.

The loneliness Clare felt before she met Zoe, or later, on days like
the day of the hog-killing, when Zoe was not around, was hard to
bear. There was an absolute stillness about the country. There were no
sounds which were not heard day after day. Roosters crowing—not
just in the dawn but at steady intervals until nightfall. Hens complain-
ing to each other and scratching around the dirt yard. Dogs barking
now and again—at nothing, at a passerby a mile away. Sound traveled
far in St. Elizabeth.

The steady noise of the river was mixed with the voices of women
at the river—on Mondays, the washerwomen. As she sat on the porch,
Clare could hear their voices and the water split by the slap-slap of
cloth against rock. On Saturdays, the voices of the butcher's wife and
her daughters traveled up the hill, as they cleaned the tripe the butcher
would later carry from yard to yard, along with other meat, peddling
Sunday dinner. At about two o'clock on each Saturday afternoon Clare
saw him, trudging up the hill—over one shoulder, a sack of freshly
killed and freshly cleaned meat, over the other, his scales, on which
he balanced the flesh on one tray against small brass weights on the
other. "How you do, Miss Clare; beg you call Miss Mattie fe me." Each

time he said the same words. Each time Clare fetched her grandmother, who appeared and pondered the contents of Mas Wilbur's
sack and decided whether they would have goat or beef or pork—or
the usual Sunday chicken.

There were only a few tasks which Miss Mattie allowed Clare to
take part in. She was too young. She was not a girl who should be
spending too much of her time on chores. Her childhood did not need
to be filled up with work. All these things her grandmother said. But
Miss Mattie let Clare help her with the preparations for her Sunday
meeting. And together they prepared coffee.

In the coolness of the early morning or the early evening, Clare set
off with her basket down into the coffee piece and returned with the
basket filled to the brim with crimson-red berries. Within each berry
were two beans, and the process of making coffee had to do with re-
leasing the beans from the hull of the berry. Out back, near to the
outhouse, was a long and wide pavement made of cement, called a
barbecue. Clare poured the berries from her basket onto the barbecue,
taking care to separate them so that each berry would catch the sun
equally. Over the next few days the berries blanched in the sunlight,
and Clare raked them with a bamboo rake now and then, turning the
still-red sides to the light—crimson gradually disappearing until the
berries were colorless.

Once blanched, Miss Mattie set aside an afternoon to attend to the
rest of the process. She and Clare built an open fire near the barbecue
and roasted the berries until they were almost black. They took turns,
shaking a flat steel pan over the fire, steadily back and forth across the
flames, until the heat accomplished its purpose and the coffee was
ready for pounding and threshing.

Miss Mattie brought forth a huge wooden pestle and mortar—the
mortar deep and worn and scarred, the pestle shiny and smooth. She
fixed the mortar firmly between her legs and pounded until the coffee
was fine enough to pass through a wire sieve. Her brown and muscled
upper arms worked the pestle against the beans, each stroke seeming
to release more of the smell of the roasted coffee, bits of hull flying
out and sticking to apron and her hair. She sweated and grunted
from the work of pounding but did not stop until every last bean was
crushed fine. Clare's job at this stage was to pass the ground coffee
through the sieve, discarding the pieces of hull, and to store the coffee in Golden Syrup and Ovaltine tins—for the use of the family and

people around who did not grow their own coffee trees. When their task was finished, Miss Mattie took some of the fresh coffee and filled a tightly woven cotton sack with it. She immersed the sack in boiling water for a time, and the two workers drank enamel mugs of hot coffee and condensed milk around the dining-room table as their reward. The smell and taste of the new coffee, mixed with the sweet thickness of the milk, was a pleasure almost impossible to bear.

But grandmother and granddaughter did not do this often—"There is too much to do on this place, and no rest for the weary."—and for the most part, Clare's time in the country, until she met Zoe, was spent waiting to return to Kingston.

Miss Mattie sent to Breezy Hill to ask Miss Ruthie whether Zoe would be her granddaughter's playmate. Zoe was at the porch steps the next morning and came many mornings over the next two months.

The two girls walked the roads barefoot, and used the mud from the roadbed to make dishes and cups for their tea parties. But the creation of vessels from clay was the real aim of their activity, and the tea parties never came to an end, in fact were barely begun, because they were interrupted by a desire to climb a star apple or custard apple tree—and the girls soon abandoned what was really a town pursuit for what the country held for them. They crushed blossoms from bushes and mixed them with water, and with the dye drew patterns on the branches where they sat together and dripped from the juices of the apples. They said they were making secret totems, in a language only they could decipher, a pictographic system like the Mayans had invented. Clare repeated to Zoe all that Boy had told her about the Mayans and Aztecs and Incas, and these ancient peoples became part of their games.

Sometimes they climbed into the high branches of the ackee and picked some of the red-podded fruit. Concealed within the fleshy yellow pouches which were edible was a sprinkling of red powder—"deadly poison." Zoe explained what Mr. Powell had told her; that Jamaicans were the only island people daring enough to eat the ackee. They scraped the poison into old condensed milk tins and hid it in a secret place for use against their enemies. Secrecy was something they held between themselves. Enemies was an abstract term which they usually put no face to.

They found an old piece of red cloth in Miss Mattie's sewing basket and used it to taunt the bull Miss Mattie kept tethered by the river, until poor Old Joe nearly went crazy with frustration and they laughed and jumped in the river and splashed him until he retreated to his guinea grass patch.

In the beginning they were shy with one another. Clare was afraid that Zoe would not like her—would resent Miss Mattie's request, tied as it was to Miss Ruthie and her daughters squatting on her grandmother's land. Although Miss Mattie would never have mentioned such a thing. Zoe didn't really mind, though; Miss Mattie's invitation got her out of keeping house so much and having to play all the time with her younger sister, because Miss Ruthie kept her girls close to their yard. And Miss Ruthie explained that it was little enough they could do in return for their shelter, and land which gave them a livelihood.

But Zoe did not know what to expect—realizing that Clare was a town girl and fair enough to be taken for *buckra*. "One big fat buckra papa she have," Miss Ruthie told her daughter. "But she mama a decent woman." Suppose Clare thought she was really somebody— suppose she looked down on Zoe because she was the pickney of a marketwoman? Zoe would just have to wait and see—something Miss Ruthie was always telling her anyway.

For Clare, Zoe would be the first girl she would know from Kitty's home. Kitty had told her about the friendships she had had with girls in her childhood—how these were the friends she remembered. All the friends she would ever need, she said.

The two girls—who had lived all their lives in Jamaica and had been taught about themselves not only by Miss Ruthie and Kitty, but by Lewis Powell and Boy Savage—were well aware that there were differences between them, of course. Had it not been for the differences, the friendship probably would not have begun in the first place. But in their friendship the differences could become more and more of a background, which only rarely they stumbled across and had to confront. They had childhood—they had make-believe. They had a landscape which was wild and real and filled with places in which their imaginations could move.

Their friendship over these years was expanded and limited in this wild countryside—the place where they kept it. It was bounded by bush and river and mountain. Not by school or town—and felt somewhat free of the rules of those places. They could walk up a hillside together without once speaking. They could take a machete and carve a ball from the root of the bamboo plant by the road and play hard catch—trying to burn the palms of each other's hands, trying to hold out until the other one yelled "Stop!" and ran to squeeze some juice from an aloe plant on her hand-middle. They did not yet question who each was in this place—if the need to question was there, it remained in the back of their minds. For now they spoke to each other through games and codes, secrets and enemies.

But there were times, as they got closer, when they were able to speak more from their hearts, drop some of the games, and make promises neither one would be able to keep. Like having a school together, when they became teachers. Or a free clinic, when they became doctors. Just another form of make-believe.

This was a friendship—a pairing of two girls—kept only on school vacations, and because of their games and make-believe might have seemed to some entirely removed from what was real in the girls' lives. Their lives of light and dark—which was the one overwhelming reality. But this friendship also existed close to the earth, in a place where there were no electric lights, where water was sought from a natural source, where people walked barefoot more often than not. This place was where Zoe's mother worked for her living and where Kitty Freeman came alive. To the girls, for a time, this was their real world—their true plane of existence for two months of the year when all other things fell outside.

The real world—that is, the world outside country—could be just as dreamlike as the world of make-believe—on this island which did not know its own history.

~~~

On another plane, in Clare's school in Kingston, there were girls as dark as Zoe, like the girls at the bus stop Clare had called "inhuman." These dark girls were at St. Catherine's mostly on scholarship—but then Clare herself was a scholarship student. Boy was unable to keep up the payments; it was the only way she could stay in school. For Clare it was different, though—and that was part of the confusion she felt—part of the split within herself. There had been an incident the previous October which Clare would never forget, and which had given her a clue to the difference between herself and the other scholarship students. Color. Class. But not in those words.

The entire school—mistresses and students—were standing at prayers, at attention, in the gymnasium which was also an auditorium and chapel, and the headmistress, Miss Haverhill, was leading them in the school hymn: "God of Our Fathers, Whose Almighty Hand, Leads Forth in Beauty All the Starry Band." The hymn which began with the organ imitating a trumpet call. As all sweated under the zinc roof—the mistresses in their light cotton dresses, the girls in their heavy gabardine uniforms, waiting for an end to the hymn, a dark girl had an epileptic seizure. She was, or had been, standing not far from Clare, when suddenly she was face-down on the floor of cold stone, cracking her nose and cheekbones on the flagstones with incredible force, as if all the energy in her body was drawn together in this one exertion. As it must have been. The girl's name was Doreen Paxton; her mother was a maid for an American family living in Barbican and Doreen lived with her grandmother on Mountainview Road, not far from the Tabernacle. Doreen was a genius at the western roll, the teachers said, and every games-day leaped and flew over the high-jump bar beyond the heights charted by the girls of Immaculate Conception. Her deep-brown body now rolled and jerked on the gymnasium floor and the girls moved back to give her room. The headmistress sang louder, as if to convey to the girls that they must not stop, must work to cover the sound of Doreen's skull and face hitting against rock, and the low groans coming from inside her. But the voices of the other girls, which had thinned considerably in volume, could not mask the noise—and the headmistress's spindly second soprano moved forward almost in a solo, with only small support from the other mistresses.

Finally, Miss Maxwell, the tall and herself-dark physical education teacher, came over and knelt beside Doreen. She drew the cloth belt from her white tennis shorts and slid it between the girl's teeth, clamping it to make sure that Doreen did not swallow her tongue. When the seizure was over, Miss Maxwell, in one smooth and graceful motion, lifted Doreen from the ground and carried her to a tumbling mat in a corner of the gym. She covered the girl with a few towels so she wouldn't take a chill, and sat beside her until she came out of the deep sleep which follows a seizure. A sleep which wipes away the memory of what has happened to you.

When the child awoke, Miss Maxwell had to tell her what had happened, that her grandmother had been called, and there was now, or would be, some trouble about her scholarship. Before she left the gym, after she gave her benediction, Miss Haverhill had conferred with Miss Maxwell and instructed her to tell Doreen "as gently as possible" that she could no longer represent the name of St. Catherine with her western roll, and so her funds would have to be stopped. The headmistress had stressed that Miss Maxwell convey this information as soon as possible—but it was hard for her to bring herself to say all this, and hard for the girl to take it all in. Doreen's body ached from its violent contact with the stone floor. Her head burned and throbbed from the explosion of the seizure. She was exhausted and scared. She was not certain what had happened to her, and did not know why. Her cheekbones were already beginning to swell and to distort the planes of her young brown face. Her nose pained her about the bridge and her eyes were darkening. Miss Maxwell left her there for a minute to take in what she had said, and went to the school gate to meet the old lady who was Doreen's grandmother and tell her what had happened. She took grandmother and granddaughter up to U.C.W.I. hospital so Doreen could be examined, because Miss Haverhill was concerned that the school might be liable for any lasting injury. The old lady—in her best dress of navy cotton with tiny white spots on it—sat in the backseat of Miss Maxwell's small Austin and wept and prayed alternately. "Wha' fe do? Lord Jesus, wha' fe do?" She repeated again and again. Terrified that her granddaughter might be damaged in some irreparable way and well aware of the mystical and strange nature of epilepsy which would shame them, she prayed and cried and cried and prayed, until the words became a chant. Miss Maxwell, whose own grandmother was not unlike this old lady weeping and chanting in her car, tried her best to explain to Mrs. Paxton that Doreen would most likely be all right but that St. Catherine's felt the pressure of the scholarship would be too much for a girl subject to fits.

Clare knew nothing of these details, only that when she asked Miss Maxwell about the incident, she was told by the gym teacher that Doreen would not be returning to school because she was an epileptic and might be a "danger" to herself. And like Claudia Lewis, it soon seemed to many of the girls that she never actually existed at all. Her name was not mentioned in the school after that.

But Clare could not erase from her mind what had happened in the gymnasium that morning. She would not forget the banging of Doreen's head against the floor, the way her mouth had foamed, and her eyeballs had rolled back in her head—the deep brown disappeared and all you could see were the whites. She came back from school that day and asked her parents about fits and they told her about epilepsy. A terrible disease. An incurable disease. Boy recounted the stories of the famous epileptics of history—like Dostoevsky and Julius Caesar.

Kitty told her that epilepsy could travel through families—although the Freemans were uncontaminated. It was a curse—Kitty said. A stigma—Boy insisted.

Something else about the morning bothered Clare, and she turned to Kitty.

"But, Mother, how come no one came forward to help except Miss Maxwell? No one came forward at all. They acted like it wasn't happening."

"Well, dear, Miss Maxwell is trained in first aid, and the other teachers were probably afraid that they would do the wrong thing."

"But even when the fit was over, none of them went to see if Doreen was okay."

"Clare, you know how Englishwomen are—they think that they are ladies; they are afraid of the least little sign of sickness or anything like that."

To Clare's mind a lady was someone who dressed and spoke well. A lady was a town creature. A lady often had people in her home where they talked about the theater or books. Above all, a lady was aloof—Clare knew all of these criteria from the Hollywood movies she saw and the lessons of her teachers. They did think they were ladies. They taught her to drop her patois and to speak "properly." *Proper* was a word they used very often. Fountain pens were proper, ballpoint pens were not. Laced-up oxfords were proper, sandals were not. Woolen berets were proper, panama hats were not. The ladies at her school disdained corporal punishment, which they thought suitable only for state schools, and preferred wrongdoers to sit beneath the lignum vitae in the quad and ponder their sins. In silence. Ladies, Clare had been taught, did not speak in a familiar manner to people beneath their station. Those with the congenital defect of poverty—or color.

So these women did not come forward because they were ladies. That was simple.

Of course, Clare held an unspoken question about Kitty. What would she have done? Kitty was certainly no "lady"—she had no pretensions to be one. Kitty was more comfortable speaking patios and walking through the bush. She confined her social world to St. Elizabeth and an occasional lunch with the women who worked beside her at the hotel desk. If Boy insisted, she would have a few of his business acquaintances in, and dress herself up, and be polite to them; but for the most part, Boy entertained his business acquaintances in hotel lounges without his wife.

Lady or not, Clare knew that Kitty would not have come forward. Even though Doreen was the color of the people to whom Kitty was tender. Later, when Clare thought about Anne Frank, and Anne's mother, Clare would have similar thoughts to those she had now. What was missing. In her own mother. In Anne Frank's mother. In the mistresses who only stood there, trying to turn their eyes from the sight of Doreen smashing against the stones. And the sight of the dark Miss Maxwell tending her and carrying her across the floor. As Kitty Hart's mother hid her under the mattresses. What made some women able to come forward, and others only to hold back?

Clare's mind got caught in a tangle with her mother and the mistresses and she didn't realize that the creole and white teachers at St. Catherine's were different from Kitty in ways other than lady ways. At the bottom—as it usually was—was race and shade. It was easy to lose sight of color and all that went with it within the imitation-English quadrangle of brick buildings. A school with a tuck shop that sold English sweeties and copies of *School-Friends*, stories of English girls in English boarding-schools. It was so easy to lose sight of color when you were constantly being told that there was no "colour problem" in Jamaica. Or anywhere in the Empire, for that matter—Her Majesty's Government had all that under control. Apartheid, for example, was only a way of keeping the peace—Black people in South Africa, the geography mistress told them, had as equal chances as the whites. Just like in Jamaica.

Light and dark were made much of in that school. It was really nothing new in Jamaica—but, as in the rest of the society, it was concealed behind euphemisms of talent, looks, aptitude. Just as Kitty had called Clare's teachers "ladies" when she knew full well that they were damned narrow-minded racists as she told herself—that was why they let that child nearly kill herself on the rockstone. Color was diffuse and hard to track at St. Catherine's, entering the classrooms as seating arrangements, disciplinary action, entering the auditorium during the casting of a play. The shadows of color permeated the relationships of the students, one to one. When the girls found out that Victoria Carter, whom everyone thought was the most beautiful girl in school, was the daughter of a Black man who worked as a gardener and an Englishwoman who had settled in Jamaica, her position in their eyes was transformed, and girls who had been quite intimidated by her, now spoke about her behind her back.

~~~

In the town, in the school, girls talked and talked about one another. Disagreements were always settled by talk and gossip and raised voices; and punishment between the girls was meted out by sending someone to Coventry—the English name for the silent treatment.

In country, between Zoe and Clare, talk or silence was not their primary means of settling their disagreements. They fought each other.

Their battles usually occurred when the differences-already-there surfaced in such a way that they couldn't be avoided or dismissed or passed over by a suggestion from one girl to the other that they retreat into the bush or dive into the river or pretend their argument was only part of a game. These surfacings were sometimes suggested by seemingly trivial things, othertimes by things which started out trivial and then moved out to become things of importance.

Their second summer together, when they were eleven, Clare was sent to country with a new bathsuit. And Zoe had asked to borrow it. Not to wear it swimming but to try it on. Clare at once refused her friend, falling back without thinking on her grandmother's instructions.

"No, man; dis is fe me suit. Grandma say wunna is to wear the other one."

"Oh, man, let me try on the sint'ing, nuh?"

"No, man, Grandma say no."

"What you mean 'Grandma say no'—is wunna say no."

"A no fe me to decide. Grandma e'en told me."

"Wunna is friend?"

"Lord, have mercy, Zoe, I can't help it."

"What you mean? Wunna is one wuthless cuffy, passing off wunnaself as buckra."

"Me no is cuffy."

"Wunna is fe true. One true sheg-up cuffy."

They wrangled on and on. Then Clare struck first, clapping Zoe at the side of her head, boxing her ears and knocking her down. This dispute began on the porch of Miss Mattie's house and they fought themselves down the dirt road toward the river. Zoe chased after Clare and kicked her in the shins. Clare moved fast, grabbed Zoe's foot and pulled, so Zoe fell over backways. Then Clare ran toward the river and Zoe caught up with her as she was balancing over the rocks. Zoe pushed her down in the water until Clare sputtered and gasped for "peace."

"Okay. Okay. I give wunna peace, but only if wunna say wunna is sorry and that wunna is one true cuffy and stingy as one dog."

Clare recited all these things to her friend, and they got up and turned back up the hill to the house, where Clare gave Zoe the new bathsuit, and told her she could keep it. And Zoe refused.

"A fe wunna bathsuit. Me have me own."

Later, at the river where they had gone to swim, Clare got a flame-red blossom of hibiscus and put it behind Zoe's left ear and told her friend that she should be a princess and that Clare would be the prince and lead an army of red ants, biting ants, which were now on their way, marching toward them, in an attack on their enemies.

She thought—or needed to think—that they had a common enemy. She dressed Zoe in flowers and palm fronds and sat her on a high rock, as if to make up for the bathsuit incident she wanted to forget.

⁓

"But, Mama, why she no let me try on she bathsuit?"

"Lord, child, why wunna worry wunnaself. She no buckra child? De buckra people dem is fe dem alone."

"But Clare is fe me friend."

"Clare is de granddaughter of Miss Mattie. Dem is rich people. Dem have property. Dem know say who dem is. She can't be wunna true friend, sweetie. Fe she life is in Kingston. She no mus' have friends in Kingston. In fe she school. Wunna is she playmate. No fool wunnaself."

"No, Mama, we be friends."

"Den why she no let wunna borrow she bathsuit? Sweetie, mus' not get too close to buckra people dem."

Chapter Fourteen

When the two girls talked, their talk much of the time focused on what they considered the world outside the country and how strange it was. This outside world did not consist of Kingston—

for Kingston was rarely mentioned by either one of them. They meant the big world. The world which was made up of England and America.

Clare's uncle, who came down to the country sometimes while she was there, to shoot birds and to visit his eldest son, Joshua, ordered a newspaper which came bundled every month from England. It was a cheap tabloid, filled with scandal, stories of the royal family, and pictures of white women half-naked. After he left, Clare and Zoe would take it with them into the bush, away from Miss Mattie, who disapproved of it entirely—"a wicked, wicked t'ing"—and sit under a guava tree and read the stories aloud.

One particular afternoon, in the summer they were eleven, the same summer as the bathsuit incident, two stories caught their attention. In one, a doctor in Edinburgh reported that there was a rare disease which only girls could contract, in which they were gradually turned into men. The disease was not life-threatening—the paper said—just irrevocable. And there was no cure. The doctor, when interviewed, said they were not working on a cure. The disease was rare; only a few cases had been reported. While Clare and Zoe viewed the world outside country and outside Jamaica as strange, they did not doubt that the newspaper reported fact—and this particular fact terrified them.

"Lord, have mercy," Zoe said. "Imagine, wunna could tun into one man, and wunna mama cannot do no-t'ing. Wunna would have fe travel far far away and become one other smaddy."

Clare said that this was more like a curse than a disease, and worried about the possibility that either one of them would be seized by it. It was as though the newspaper story addressed them directly. They became the only girls in the world who might become contaminated.

"What would we do?" Zoe asked. "I would be so 'shamed."

Clare thought. "Well, if only one of us got the disease, then the other one could marry her and promise never to tell a soul."

"Don't make game, man, gal can't marry gal."

The two of them worried for at least a week afterwards that they had the disease or that one of them would get it and pass it on to the other. They searched their bodies for signs, and tried to figure out what the signs would be. Would they begin by acting differently—they thought about the mannerisms some men had. Walking in a certain way. Stroking their chins—Mr. Powell did that when he was considering something. Spitting against the wind. Would they act differently at first? Or would they begin to grow one of those things they called "pepsis"? What would they do with a pepsi? They were only just beginning to develop, were waiting around for their "monthlies" to start—and now this.

The second story in the paper scared them as much as the first one had. It was about a five-year-old girl in Peru who had given birth to a baby boy. Zoe and Clare knew about the process by which women became pregnant—it had to do with the pepsi of the man and the "pussy" of the woman. But neither girl could imagine this act taking place in the pussy of a five-year-old girl. This was a girl younger than their sisters, who were younger than they were. They knew that the female had to have her monthlies before the pepsi could take effect in the pussy—they had never heard of a five-year-old girl having monthlies ever. Although the writer of the article reported that in "tropical countries" girls menstruated earlier than in "temperate countries," neither Zoe nor Clare had yet, and they were skeptical about this statement of science. But they focused their attention on the presence or absence of monthlies in the life of a five-year-old girl; neither wanted to think about the exact method by which this little girl became pregnant. They knew about rape—Miss Ruthie and Miss Mattie had counseled them long and hard about this. Confusing them with stern advice that they should watch themselves around men because they might tempt the men without knowing they were tempting them: "Don't get too old before your time." That was one warning.

But neither girl had thought that such little children could be raped—or that anyone would want to do this. It seemed to them so unbelievably cruel. A little girl's pussy was so tiny—Clare envisioned her grandfather's penis—and saw a tiny opening being torn apart by the pepsi of a grown man. But she stopped herself—and couldn't bring herself to tell Zoe—who was having similar thoughts. Zoe remembered a girl in school who had trouble holding her water—there had been some whispers about her—and now Zoe quietly made a connection, and kept it to herself.

This was such a hard thing to consider.

Both knew about incest. They knew that Mas Freddie who drove LIGHTNING had given his daughter a baby, or so people said; and people said it in exactly that way—but his daughter Rose was a grown woman, and the two of them had lived together in a small house on a hillside since her mother's death. And the community depended on Mas Freddie and his truck, so little was made of it.

The girls read and re-read the story and found there were no details at all about who the baby's father might have been. The reporter even implied that because Peru was a Catholic country, there might have been *no* father at all. The story tried to turn what had been conceived and borne in violence and tragedy into something of mystery and devotion. A virgin birth in the Andes. The birth of a baby to a five-year-old girl became the story—not the act which had produced the baby, not the five-year-old body which had carried a being inside, nor any speculation of what might happen to either child.

The Virgin Mary, the article concluded, had been fourteen when God had impregnated her.

These two stories, the mythic disease and the mythic birth, became connected in the girls' minds—one becoming in the end as impossible to believe as the other. Both things appeared to Clare and Zoe caused by some mysterious force over which they would have no control at all. Two unwanted and sudden disasters which would change their lives totally. Two visitations about which they could do nothing. The only power they had was to burn the newspaper—and that is what they did.

Which would be worse, they asked each other: to turn into a man or to become a mother at five, or eleven, or fourteen. Both things seemed beyond their grasp and it didn't much matter which they would choose, because it didn't seem to be theirs to choose. The filament which bound the two stories—that their bodies might not belong to them—tightened around the girls. But this was the world beyond Jamaica, Clare said. Forgetting about Mas Freddie and his daughter Rose and about her grandmother's warnings—and not knowing about the girl in Mr. Powell's school who could not hold her water.

As she walked by herself one evening on her way back to Breezy Hill, Zoe thought again about the girl in her class, whom she sometimes led to the river and washed off and dried alongside her clothes on a rock in the sun, and how the girl sniffled with shame and shivered against the light.

When Zoe got to her yard, Miss Ruthie was bent over a patch of gunga peas, gently squeezing the pods to see if the peas were ready to be picked. Zoe always felt safe with her mama—if Miss Ruthie was around nothing bad would happen to her.

"Mama, wunna know de pickney of Miss Et'el? She the one who all the time peepee in Mr. Powell class?"

"Yes, me know she."

"How come she cannot hold she water? How come she all the time peepee on sheself?"

Miss Ruthie took Zoe's hands and looked hard at her, into her eyes.

"Well, Sweetie . . . when she was small . . . I t'ink 'bout seven or eight years she was. Some boy dem lick she down—she did catch dem teefing some guava from down a river—dem did lick she down and dem did vi-o-late she. Poor little t'ing. But she mama should tell she not fe walk alone. Gal pickney no mus' stay by dem yard."

"Yes, Mama."

"Dem never did catch de boy dem. Some smaddy say it was dem red boy from Lynch Vale, but me no know. Sweetie, you jus' stay in dis here yard and Miss Mattie yard and don't walk far alone. De boys dem, 'specially de red boy and de buckra boy, can do all manner of wicked t'ing."

"What if dem had catch de boy?"

"Dey not gwan tek de word of one little Black child pon dem."

"Is not fair, Mama."

"No, Sweetie, is not fair."

~~~

It had been from Zoe that Clare learned what "monthlies" were. Kitty had not told her, nor would she; she had instructed Boy to tell his daughter about it, and he wasn't able to either. He had driven Clare for miles and miles one afternoon in Kingston, way up into the foothills of the Blue Mountains, around and around, and he couldn't bring himself to say anything except that women suffered terribly in childbirth and so Clare should always respect Kitty. He parked the car on a bluff, from which they could see the lights of cruise ships docked in the harbor, and told his daughter that boys were after only one thing—he didn't say what this thing was—so Clare should keep her distance because it could be dangerous and a girl could be easily "ruined." That was his word, and that was all he said—and she didn't ask further because she could tell from the heaviness in the car that she would learn nothing else, or anything she could use. She just let him have his say and waited for the moment when he would start the car again and they would return home.

It was menstruation which concerned Clare more than sex between men and women, pregnancy and childbirth. Menstruation appeared to her as the culmination of the process that was happening within and without her girl's body and she wanted to understand it for what it was—and what it would mean in her life. She had a sense of it as something which would allow no turning back—a "milestone," she called it. But she had a sense of it as a sweetness—a truly private piece of life—like the inscription in Greek on an award she had won at school: "Your possession forever." She had read about menstruation in the *Diary of a Young Girl*, because Anne Frank had written about it, in a secretive, unto-herself way; as though it was something she had achieved.

Kitty referred to menstruation as her "friend"—which seemed to Clare, once she had broken her mother's code, a beautiful thing to call it.

When she took off her school blouse in the evenings to tidy for dinner with her parents, she stroked her nipples and found them tender but also wanting of her strokes. The stroking, back and forth and up and down made her pussy warm. She would raise an arm and run the other hand under her armpit, playing with the hairs, then across her breasts, and into and through the lips of her vagina, where her fingers settled and gently rubbed. She never consciously thought about doing this, about whether it was right or wrong. She knew that she was in the middle of something which would change her for good and was eager for the menstruation which would complete these feelings of change and growth.

She knew the feelings of her body and the feelings expressed by Anne Frank about menstruation, but she was ignorant about the details. Her teachers at St. Catherine's only hinted around the fact of menstruation but said nothing of substance—their most obvious act excusing from class a shaky or sweaty girl now and again. When Clare asked Dorothy to explain the physical parts of monthlies to her, Dorothy refused, saying this was a sint'ing between mother and daughter, and that she would get into trouble if she took it away from Miss Kitty.

So Clare went to Zoe and Zoe explained what she knew. That periods—as some people called them—were times when a woman bled from her pussy and it could hurt but it meant that a woman could have a baby. The baby began when the man's pepsi shot something inside the woman's pussy, which started an egg—"A tiny, tiny little t'ing, not like a chicken's egg a-tall."—developing into a baby. A girl must mind that no man's pepsi came into her or else she would get a baby.

Clare never asked Zoe whether she stroked herself in her pussy or across her chest or squeezed her own nipples. There were places in her parents' house Clare could do this secretly—but Zoe lived in one room with her mother and sister. Clare didn't mention to her friend the sweet and deep feeling when she did these things, nor the salty taste of her own moisture on her fingertips.

My company is going far
And I am left alone
My company is going far
And I am left alone
My company
My company
My company is going far

—traditional.

Chapter Fifteen

On one particular morning in September—the year the girls were twelve—Clare got up earlier than her grandmother. It was about five a.m. when she woke, dressed, and went into the dining room and opened the closet where her uncle kept his rifle and a box of shells. Her grandmother, in her long white nightgown and long gray braid, snored on as Clare gently raised herself from the doublebed they shared. In the dining room, she unlocked the cabinet door, removed the gun and ammunition, loaded the gun and locked the cabinet back again, replacing the key in its hiding place, a tin tray on a high shelf. Then she left by the back way to meet Zoe at the graves beyond the coffee piece.

The morning was cool and barely light. Walking through the coffee piece in the not-yet dawn, it became darker, as the shade trees which hovered over the bushes cut out any light there might have been. It was always dark down there, even when everywhere else was bright sunlight. As she walked she could hear the rats that lived on the red berries running ahead of her through the densely planted bushes—which had been part of her great-grandmother Judith's livelihood, and legacy. Clare, at those times when she gathered the coffee for Miss Mattie, was usually frightened by this noise, but this morning she carried a loaded rifle, and she felt dangerous. No other sound was there, except for the occasional rustle or squawk of a chicken dropping from its roost in one of the shade trees. There was a deep musty smell which traveled through the darkness of the coffee piece. Of leaves and manure and eggshells and fishbones and vegetables her grandmother used to thicken the earth. Above this smell was the thin sharp scent of urine, because Miss Mattie emptied their chamberpots near to the edge of the planting. All these things rotted silently in the moisture and darkness of this part of the property where the earth was most damp.

At the end of the coffee piece, about fifty yards from the house, and near to the almond tree were Clare had talked with Mad Hannah on the day of the hog-killing, were two graves of former landowners. Two above-ground graves that resembled the graves of Miss Judith and Mas Samuel, but were much older. People around said that the graves were as old as slavery times—and the names, of a planter and his wife, had been erased by rains, and the spaces where the names had been, obliterated by a heavy green mold. Some people said that the planter and his wife had been killed by a raiding party of Maroons, but no one was sure.

Zoe was sitting at the edge of one of these graves, honing her machete on a stone as Clare approached and waved to her.

On Angel's Hill, across the river and up the slope, was a wild pig who had lived in the underbrush for what people said was at least twenty years, but no one really knew. No one had ever been able to kill him, although once someone caught him sidewise with a bullet, so he could be recognized by a small scar on his snout, in the shape of a teardrop. The pig was named Massa Cudjoe and was the descendent of what had been the predominant form of animal life on the island before the conquerors came, outnumbering even the Arawaks, who would not kill them. There had been thousands and thousands of wild pigs, until the planters began to shoot them, and the Maroons stalked them for food. The Maroons turned the hunting of the wild pig into a ritual, searching for the animal only at certain times of the year and arming themselves with nothing but machetes and spears. It was a man's ritual—the women took part when the pig was brought back to the settlement. The women had devised a method of curing the meat without the use of salt. The parts they did not cure they buried in a deep pit filled with red-hot charcoals and covered the meat and the coals with earth. The result was called "jerked pork"—and was considered a great delicacy.

But even with the hunting of the Maroons and the clearing of habitat by the planters, the main enemy of the pig was not man; it was the mongoose—a small and almost fearless little beast the sugar planters imported from India to destroy the snakes who lived in the canefields. The mongoose was considered the natural enemy of the cobra—and although there were no cobras in Jamaica, there were other poisonous snakes, as well as boa constrictors. The planters panicked because some of their cane-cutters were being killed off, and others were refusing to work the fields. At first the landowners tried running fire through the fields, but this was not entirely successful, so they sent for the mongoose, who came and destroyed all species of snake on the island.

The mongoose was gray, with coarse and shaggy hair and a bushy tail, its body growing to a length between two and four feet. He was smart, built low to the ground like a weasel, and very fast. The bushmaster was one of the snakes which served him as prey. The bushmaster was a viper, the largest venomous snake encountered in the New World—ranging from eight to twelve feet long. His skin was gray and brown and formed into a diamond pattern. The creatures met one another against low brush, whose colors protected them. The mongoose approached the bushmaster, moving himself forward and back, forward and back, again and again—then feinting and dodging the strike of the snake. Triangular head arched forward from its coil of body, tensing all the muscles of its length, did the bushmaster think the little beast comical—suicidal? Did he not realize the mongoose was controlling the progress of the dance?

Persistence and speed—these kept the attack of the mongoose going until his approaches and retreats stunned the heavy, by-now-weary bushmaster. At the sign of the snake's acquiescence—a slowing of reflex reflected in glassed-over eyes—the mongoose struck once more, faster and more deftly than before, not retreating this time, but seizing the snake's head in his jaws and cracking the skull between his teeth. Devouring the head—pockets of venom and all.

People thought the mongoose knew of a secret root, an antidote to the poison of the snake. They thought the mongoose cultivated the root in the deep bush, and that the root made the mongoose gradually immune to venom. But there was no such root: the mongoose behaved as he did neither from immunity nor by instinct. He was taught this behavior by the mother mongoose, and she lost several babies to snakebite before the others mastered the technique.

The mongoose in Jamaica multiplied rapidly after all the snakes were dead, and then he began to kill the chickens, and the birds, and the wild pigs.

He was smart enough not to attack a wild pig at any time when the pig might retaliate and spear the mongoose with his tusks. The pig did not follow a ritual as did the bushmaster—and the mongoose could not depend on any delicate dance back and forth. The pig would simply charge, a huge beast trampling and skewering any small mammal in its path. So the mongoose waited patiently and stalked the pig until he found a lair where a pig lay on her side, attending to herself as she brought forth her babies. He approached the pig in silence, slinking through underbrush, and watched as each baby slid from her opening slick with birth. One by one she delivered her babies, and one by one the mongoose seized them and ate them. When the pig had finished and was looking to fasten her babies to her teats and eat the placenta which had followed on their birth, she found no babies, no placenta, nothing at all—and the mongoose had long since disappeared back into the underbrush. People said you could hear the bellows of her loss sound through the mountains of the countryside— that was how they could tell that Massa Mongoose was close by, and they took precautions against him—penning their fowl and gathering up their eggs. And the pig wandered in confusion—with filled breasts and no babies to suckle them.

This was the nature of the mongoose—of all the animals in Jamaica he seemed to be the true survivor. It could be said, of course, that since the white landowners had imported the mongoose in the first place, they were to blame for the deaths of the wild pigs, chickens, birds, and snakes; but people usually blamed this swift and angry little creature, who was nocturnal and seldom seen.

⁓

The hunt for the wild pig was Clare's idea. But neither she nor Zoe, who had gone along, saying little, had thought about the reality of it, at least not past taking the rifle and ammunition, and walking up Angel's Hill to cut their way through to the pig's lair with a machete. No doubt the experience of the hog-killing—when she had been told absolutely, by the boys, by the dressed-up women, by Miss Mattie, by Mad Hannah, just who she was to be in this place—had something to do with Clare's wish to capture and kill Massa Cudjoe. Maybe somewhere she had even thought about roasting and feasting on his penis and testicles. Not a conscious thought—she had said that the act of Ben and Joshua sickened her—perhaps a flash of violence in a dream. Consciously she had not weighed, had not really considered carrying through the slaughter.

She was a girl, she had taken a gun and ammunition; perhaps that was forbidden act enough. She had stepped far out of place.

Slaughter was not new to her. When Ben and his father came down to St. Elizabeth to shoot birds, they set off early and came back in the late afternoon with crocus sacks filled to bulging with nightingales, wild pigeons, and larks. Much was made of their return; Miss Mattie came onto the porch and examined the sacksful, carefully picking over the carcasses and deciding which ones she would pluck and cook for dinner, and people from round about stopped by to praise the hunters. In the evening Miss Mattie would serve some of the birds, heaping them high on her best platter. The tiny wings and legs, backs and breasts still appeared intact. Their structures of sinew and bone, their networks of muscle were emphasized where the broiling had melted away fat. Stumps of their pinfeathers stuck in their browned skin. The birds tasted of wildness and the taste and look of them turned Clare's stomach.

Chickens were different than wild birds. They were killed by Miss Mattie or Kitty. Chickens were stupid. Once their period of egg-laying finished, their deaths became women's work. Carried out after church, quickly and cleanly, barehanded, and usually out of sight. Their bodies were not trophies with the smell of a wild habitat about them. They were Bessie or Vinnie, an old fowl, known by her gold speckles or her peeled-neck, who had outlasted her day-to-day use and was ready to become Sunday dinner. The deaths of chickens were routine—like the blanching and roasting of coffee.

Did Clare see Miss Mattie on the porch as she and Zoe carried her the carcass of the pig? Here she was on her way to kill something wild—which had been wild for twenty years—and she had not really thought about it at all. Not the fact of the killing, not the aftermath. Only some gain she would make on her way. Kitty was in there somewhere—of course—and what Kitty would think about a daughter who could kill—and thus survive—in the wild. Kitty Hart and Anne Frank were there. And the five-year-old girlchild in Peru. And Doreen Paxton. But Clare was not ready to sort all these shadows out—and reality again gave way to a sense of make-believe.

Last Boxing Day, Joshua had made a feast for the family by buying two kids, slaughtering them with a machete, and building an enormous fire in the backyard, stewing the pieces of flesh and sharp splintery bones into curried goat. Miss Mattie had given him a length of English tweed which she would make into his first long-pants—the feast was in return for this.

Clare had eaten plateful after plateful, pouring the pieces of meat and juice over the white rice and boiled green bananas. Piling bone upon bone beside her on the ground.

After the feast Clare set out to take a walk, and just as Joshua had yelled for her to stop, had stepped forward, onto the heads of the two kids with her barefeet. Their softness came between her toes and the blood from their mouths and eyes wet her feet. The hairs from their hornless heads stuck fast with the blood. One skull had cracked against a rock when Joshua tossed it into the bush, and the bone-edge grazed her instep. She worried about infection—tetanus—lockjaw. She turned from the heads—eyes fixed and framed in blood—and moved away from Joshua into the bushes, where she threw up her dinner. Then went down to the river to wash blood, softness, and hair from her footbottoms.

She had put the goat-heads from her mind. In any case, she was going to shoot, not chop; she was on a hillside as the sun was breaking with a loaded rifle. She knew how to shoot—her uncle had taught her—just in case—for those times she and Miss Mattie and her grandfather—who was a man no longer, her uncle said—were alone on the place. She had been trained against the possibility of intruders.

⁓

The hill was wild and thick with bush. Clare and Zoe began to hack their way ahead, taking turns with the machete. They sang. They slashed. Back and forth across stalks which had never known a blade. Thick and old—impossible to cut down. Vines circled the stalks and the trunks, and wound around other vines, making the forest almost impossible to penetrate. Underfoot there were macca and cactus plants, with spines that cut through the girls' sneakers and stung their feet and ankles. They slashed between trunks of ebony and rosewood, satinwood and lignum vitae—sometimes slicing in half a wild orchid hanging from a branch, its purpled yellow-white center dropping between them, spilling water and nectar, scattering the quits which were drinking from its pouch. Clare held back the branches while Zoe slashed. Then they reversed positions and Clare worked with the cutlass. On and on, they made little headway. It was hot and still and there was no sign of any pig. The bushes were full around them, not trampled down. The bark of all the trees they saw were clean and unmarked by the scratches of tusks. They sat and rested a while. They were on the wrong track.

"Zoe, wunna t'ink we should climb a tree fe see if de pig is nearby?"

"No, man; no bother with it. Him nowhere near here."

"Wunna may be right—dere is no sign of him."

"Den why we no stop? We could tek de gun back a Miss Mattie yard and go fe a swim in de river. It too hot fe dis kind of work today."

Zoe was speaking so softly. Clare responded.

"But, man, we plan dis fe days."

Zoe sighed. "Me know, me know. But what we fe do with him when we see him. Wunna gwan crouch down and shoot him inna de eye? Inna de head? Wunna plan fe cover wunnaself with him blood fe mek ceremony? Mek one litter with palm leaves and carry him body down de hillside? T'rough de bush? Wunna mus' t'ink wunna is African, gal. Wunna mus' t'ink wunna is Maroon smaddy."

"No."

"Wunna is living inside one dream. Dese pig is fierce. Fierce and brave. Dem is proud. Him is old pig and him has lived pon dis hill fe donkey's years. Him no be easy to catch. And if we catch him, what right we have fe kill him? Dis no is game. Come, on, gal; let us give up—what you say?"

Zoe's tone was even and quiet. She had had enough of what seemed to her half-adventure and half-game. Something which for all Clare's determination seemed aimless, undefined. And wrong. Her tone seemed so grown. Clare wondered why Zoe had not said these things to her before this. She had gone along with Clare's plan of a week, but had said nothing about it, except that yes, she'd come along and help Clare cut through the bush. Zoe was not finished.

"Wunna know, wunna is truly town gal. Wunna a go back to Kingston soon now. Wunna no realize me have to stay here. Wunna no know what people dem would say if two gal dem shoot Massa Cudjoe. Dem would talk and me would have fe tek on all de contention. Dem will say dat me t'ink me is buckra boy, going pon de hill a hunt fe one pig. Or dat me let buckra gal lead me into wickedness. Or dey will say me t'ink me is Guinea warrior, not gal pickney. But wunna never reckon with dat. Wunna jus' go ahead with wunna sint'ing. Country people dem don't forget no-t'ing—fe me pickney would be traced if dem mama did do such a t'ing."

"Me not town gal. And me not buckra. Me jus' want to do something so dem will know we is smaddy."

"Wunna is town gal, and wunna papa is buckra. Wunna talk buckra. Wunna leave here when wunna people come fe wunna. Smaddy? Wunna no is smaddy already? Gal smaddy. Kingston smaddy. White smaddy. Dis place no matter a wunna a-tall, a-tall. Dis here is fe me territory. Kingston a fe wunna. Me will be here so all me life—me will be marketwoman like fe me mama. Me will have fe beg land fe me and fe me pickney to live pon. Wunna will go a England, den maybe America, to university, and when we meet later we will be different smaddy. But we is different smaddy now."

Zoe spread the word "territory" over at least six syllables, and the word and its meaning arched everything she said. Clare felt hurt. By territory, Zoe's division of it, and by Zoe's conclusion that without a doubt their lives would never be close once they reached into womanhood. This was not something that had passed between them before. Zoe seemed so certain of their fates—she sounded almost like Miss Mattie in her quiet sternness. "Cancer of the blood," Miss Mattie had said. "No one is too young to die." Why did everything seem so fixed? So unchangeable. Clare was having trouble taking in all that Zoe said; she didn't want to believe it. She wanted them to be the same.

"No, Zoe; dis is as much fe me place as fe wunna. Fe me people have been here long, long time."

"Dat is true. Fe wunna people have been here long, long time. Dem own land. Dem have meeting in dem parlor. But fe me people been here long, long time too. We even been slaves."

"But wunna no have to be marketwoman. Wunna could be teacher. We could have our school. Someday . . ."

"Chuh, gal," Zoe sucked her teeth long and slow. "Chuh, gal, wunna have fe go a teacher's college fe dat. Fe me mama no have one degga-degga shilling extra to send me a college. We is poor, man. Wunna no t'ink marketwoman is honorable business?" She pronounced the "h" and spread the word out. Ho-nor-a-ble. "Me mama is a hard-working honest woman. She know how fe grow t'ings. She know how fe bargain."

"Is not dat. Is not dat a-tall, a-tall."

"Well, gal, sometime dat is jus' de way t'ings be."

Clare fought hard not to believe all that Zoe said. But she knew that she would be leaving for Kingston soon. She knew that Kingston was the place of her existence. She felt split into two parts—white and not white, town and country, scholarship and privilege, Boy and Kitty.

Zoe knew that Clare could not really understand what she had said. She didn't think Clare had any idea of what being poor really meant. What being dark really meant. Why these things would always come between them. She cared for her playmate but she saw that she was limited. Maybe Clare would someday come into an understanding of Zoe's part of the conversation but if she did, it would take her time. Zoe had spoken from the heart. To stop the hunt she tried another way. Breaking the quiet of the bush which settled around them.

"You know, gal, de boys is different from we. Wunna know dat. Dem like fe catch wild t'ings. Anyway, not one of dem ever catch dis here wild pig. Dem is scared of him. Dem call him guardian of Angel's Hill. And him will gore any smaddy what come near. Me know say where him lair be. Is pon de tippy-top of de hill—we never gwan reach it today. Let we give up, nuh, gal? Don't be so stubborn."

Clare only half-listened to this, for her mind was back in their other conversation. Before, they would have fought—punching and kicking their way into silence. But Zoe hadn't even raised her voice. Clare's enthusiasm for the hunt slid away from her. She felt silly. Stupid.

So she half-listened and then looked at Zoe—full into her eyes. "Den why wunna come with me anyway?"

"Because one fool-fool gal like wunna need protection."

It was by now eleven, and had become a hot hot morning. The two girls decided not to go first to Miss Mattie's house. Clare would return later, hiding the gun under the house—and in the evening, when her grandmother had gone into the bedroom to plait her sleeping braid, a process which took at least a half-hour, would return the gun to the cabinet. They went straight to the river, to Annie's Hole, which was at a secluded place. And because they had no bathsuits, and no one was around, they stripped off all their clothes and splashed naked together, just as Clare had seen Ben and Joshua do—so something had been gained. This was the first time in her life that Clare had been naked with someone besides her little sister. Another girl. Another female. In her baths in this same place with Kitty each had been clothed.

Zoe's naked body was lean and muscled. Her hips were narrow and her thighs long. The patch of tight curly hair between her legs glistened in the riverwater and the sun. Clare's own body was also long. The gold of her legs and arms met the brown of Zoe as the water cascaded between them, creating a shield which served their modesty. They found a piece of Golden Guinea soap in a crevice of rock, left by last week's washerwomen, and soaped their skin and hair and splashed each other all over until the piece of soap disappeared and the bubbles and foam from their clean selves ran to another part of the river below them. They didn't stop to think that the soap had been hidden by a particular washerwoman who would have need of it next week, and would have to beg a sliver from the washerwoman at the next rock.

After their bath, the two girls lay back. Their bodies stretched against each other, supported by gray and ancient rock. Rock which was huge—and colored by the residue of soap, by streaks of the bluing the washerwomen used to make their clothes turn stark white. In some places the surface of the rock was worn smooth—by the force of the water, which was constant even in the dry season, by the beating and smacking of cotton cloth against it by the washerwomen.

In other places the gray of the rock was covered by small growths of dark green moss, which concealed cracks where water had collected and small animals lived—tiny crabs walking beneath green, black bugs skimming the surface of the water and getting tangled in the mosses. Zoe played her toes through a patch of moss and Clare dipped her fingers into another and came up with the dead body of a darning needle.

The two girls closed their eyes against the rise of the sun to noon overhead and touched hands. Brown and gold beside each other. Damp and warm. Hair curled from the heat and the wet. The warmth of the sunlight on their bodies—salty-damp.

Pussy and rass—these were the two words they knew for the space-within-flesh covered now by strands and curls of hair. Under these patches were the ways into their own bodies. Their fingers could slide through the hair and deep into the pink and purple flesh and touch a corridor through which their babies would emerge and into which men would put their thing. Right now it could belong to them. The river and the cascades of water quieted them. At the side of the bank, if they would open their eyes, they could see orange and mango trees, dwarf coconuts, and a stretch of barbed wire where Old Joe was penned.

The gun was at Clare's right side—on the dry side of the rock.

The space between them was not as neat as Zoe had perceived it. But Clare, who had never considered the subtleties of this division, could not now analyze or explain to her friend what she felt about their given identities in this society, where they met and where they diverged. Clare took all that Zoe said as an accusation that she had failed her as a friend. That was easiest. Zoe's charges became specific. Limited to Clare's own behavior in this one friendship. She had never known Zoe to be so "sensitive"—and she was surprised. And while her mind made somersaults to absolve herself of blame and to deny that so much of what Zoe said was true, she had respect for her friend for speaking as she had. Clare finally judged that, yes, she had been selfish. She had not once thought about the consequences of the hunt in Zoe's life. She had to admit to herself that she always thought the hunt was her right—her property. Somewhere she wanted to limit Zoe's statements only to that particular morning in the bush. And separate them from her life elsewhere.

Property was a word that Zoe had used. Clare's people owned property and Miss Ruthie and her daughters had to beg a piece from Miss Mattie to live on. But Clare thought that she and Zoe were removed from property as it related to deeds and acreage—in her naivete she limited the bounds of property there. After all they were girls and this was country, where Clare thought everyone crossed the lines of possession—indicated by dry walls and barbed wire—and picked fruit and cut cane from other people's land. And dug yam wherever they saw a yam hill rise. She had no sense of the nuances of ownership—of the unevenness of possession. Or that if she saw a stranger picking oranges from one of Miss Mattie's trees, this did not represent privilege but payment—for mending a break in the fence or helping with the harvest. She did not realize that it was only *she* who moved across the lines of ownership—because she was Kitty's daughter and Miss Mattie's granddaughter. And Zoe, her darker friend, her friend whose mother was a marketwoman, was only allowed along. How was it with Zoe when Clare was not around— Clare did not know because they had not spoken of it.

When Clare was not around Zoe's parameters consisted of the yard where she lived and the school of Mr. Powell. Neither Miss Ruthie nor her daughters had ever been asked inside Miss Mattie's house—had Miss Ruthie been there the day of the hog-killing, she would have stood by the guava tree in the frontyard. If Zoe was sent by her mother to Miss Mattie with a question about the land, or a piece of news she had learned in Black River, Zoe would go around the back of the small house and stand there until Miss Mattie appeared.

⁓

"Coo ya!" a voice screamed. "Two gals nekked pon de river-rock." The shout shot across the sound of the river and Clare looked up to see a man in khaki with a cutlass in his hand—a cane-cutter—who stood in front of the barbed wire and stared over the rainbows cast by the sunlight crossing through water. She reached beside her for the rifle—Zoe tried to stay her hand: "No, man, no." But Clare brushed Zoe's fingers from her wrist. She sat with the rifle across her knees, holding her knees tight together so the man could not see her, and told him to get away. He only stared at her—slightly smiling at the sight of a naked and wet girl with a rifle—trying to be dangerous while protecting her private parts from his sight. She pointed the gun at him, laying the butt at her right shoulder, the barrel on the bone of her kneecap, thighs clenched together. "Get away, you hear. This is my grandmother's land." She had dropped her patois—was speaking *buckra*—and relying on the privilege she said she did not have. The man stood stock still—maybe he thought she was crazy. He knew now she was Miss Mattie's granddaughter and it was Miss Mattie's canefields he was coming from. Maybe he didn't know what to do; he didn't want to lose the work. But even so he thought the girl comical. So he just stood there. Still pointing the gun at him, Clare began to squeeze the trigger—and at the last second before firing, jerked the gun upward and shot over the man's head, as if aiming for the coconut tree behind him.

The rifle butt came back strong and jolted her hard, pitching her backward, off-balance. She glanced at Zoe, who had turned away from her, and at that moment, before either girl could say anything, there was a scream, a bellow, and then a huge thumping of hooves toward them.

Old Joe stopped suddenly at the barbed wire, unable to reach the cool of the riverwater. Stopped in front of the girls with his left eye running down his cheek—the socket pouring blood as the egg white of his eyeball ran down his snout and onto the ground below. The guinea grass and the sensitive plants which crowded his grazing were soon covered. He was bellowing in fierce pain. Snot cascaded from his nostrils. He sank to the knees of his forelegs. The heavy blue-bottle flies began to swarm around him, gathering from nowhere—focusing on the eye-empty blood-filled socket, while two John Crows appeared and circled above him. Clare looked around for the cane-cutter—he was long gone.

The bull had been shot in the head by a bullet she had meant for no one. He was dying. Now the bellows had been replaced by moans, deep low sounds, and a terrible heaving and sighing.

"Lord, have mercy, Zoe. What we to do?" Clare spoke through her tears toward her friend.

"De bull him is dying. No mus' shoot him to end his misery."

Clare walked across the rocks, her naked body trembling—she walked right next to the bull, brushing the bluebottles away, and fired a cartridge into Old Joe's left ear. His neck snapped back, white flew from his mouth and matted in Clare's wet curls.

"I'm sorry. I'm sorry. I'm sorry." No punishment, she thought, would fit what she had done.

Chapter Sixteen

The act of putting an animal out of his misery was supposed to be an automatic act. This was what was expected if an animal was hurt past any hope of recovery. It was said to be "humane"—to bring on what was inevitable and to take away the animal's pain. Clare felt no sense of duty in shooting Old Joe the second time—no relief that he was suffering no longer. Her mind was back at the first shot and her fear of what she had done. She tried to imagine the cartridge passing through the bush—perhaps ricocheting off the trunk of a tree or the surface of a stone—until it found its target. The eye of Miss Mattie's bull. Did a bullet travel until it met flesh—it seemed that way.

A thousand things flew around in her brain, each one hard to connect to the one preceding or following it. The morning became a broken pattern of events, nothing held together, but all seemed to lead Clare to the same terrible place.

Her sleeping grandmother. The gun and ammunition. The graves. The darkness of the morning. The machete slashing against bark. Zoe. Property. Selfishness. "Gal smaddy. White Smaddy. Kingston smaddy. . . . Different smaddy." Nakedness.

She had proven what Zoe accused her of—she was at fault.

Lying beside Zoe on the rock. She had felt warm. Safe. Secluded. She felt that this was something she had wanted all along. She decided that she would never be selfish again—and believed this was possible. That she would respect Zoe's feelings more and try to see things from her side. She realized lying there on that rock that to lose Zoe's friendship would be truly a loss. She had never thought before about losing that friendship until Zoe spoke to her and the vectors of Zoe's anger threatened to cross out their closeness. Clare held on by the river that the two of them could erase difference.

She wanted on the rock to tell Zoe what she meant to her—and that she would try to be better—a better friend. In the moments before the cane-cutter startled them, she had wanted to lean across Zoe's breasts and kiss her. Just to say she was sorry. To thank Zoe for stopping her from being fool-fool.

When the cane-cutter caught them she was frightened. But the exact source of her fright she did not know. She would have known—had she stopped to think—that the cane-cutter would not have hurt her. He would soon enough have recognized by her skin and by her face that she was the granddaughter of Miss Mattie and the daughter of Kitty, whose "dead stamp" the country people said she was. He might have teased but he would have done no more. Miss Mattie was a respected woman—he would not have harmed her granddaughter. Neither would he have told Miss Mattie what he had seen.

Did Clare shoot from fear or did she shoot from shame? Did she shoot to protect Zoe or to protect herself? Or because she was angry that this man had strolled casually into their closeness? Or because she was angry that Zoe made her stop the hunt and told her things she didn't want to hear? Her thoughts were spinning, not settling.

Had she been wrong to take the gun? It seemed that way now. But when she took it she felt she had a right to it.

Clare had heard her parents talk occasionally about her uncle, Robert—not a real uncle, but a distant older cousin on her father's side—who spent a lot of his weekends in Montego Bay and lived during the week with his mother in an old frame house in Barbican. Robert was a civil servant—a light-skinned man who worked in the governor's office. The family spoke of him as "funny," but Clare was not sure what "funny" meant. She knew that Robert had caused some disturbance when he brought a dark man home from Montego Bay and introduced him to his mother as "my dearest friend." At least that was what the family said. The dearest friend was an American Negro, a sailor from a warship docked on the North Coast. There had been a lot of talk in the family then about Robert and why he had done this and if he had to have a dearest friend he might be more discreet about it. Anyway, didn't he know that American Negroes were very different from Jamaicans—the dearest friend probably led him into all this foolishness. And the dearest friend was dark—Dark American Negroes were not our kind of people a-tall, a-tall.

So this man with the wrong skin color and the wrong nationality returned to his warship and Robert went back to his weekend trips to Doctor's Cave Beach and weekdays with his mother and the governor. When the sailor—who was actually a chief petty officer—wrote to ask Robert to leave the island and "make a home together" in Brooklyn, his letters were returned.

Clare was almost eleven when this incident occurred and she went to Dorothy to ask her what "funny" meant. Dorothy responded that "it is when one smaddy is a little *off*—is one sint'ing one smaddy is born with. Him no can help himself."

"But how is he off, Dorothy?"

"Him is battyman—him want fe lay down wit' only other men. No ask me no more."

Clare didn't really understand the entire meaning of Dorothy's statement. She saw her Uncle Robert, who also happened to be her godfather, in pursuit of men to lie beside. She saw him as embarrassing himself—if this was something out of his control then he must be crazy in some way. Deficient. The next time she saw him, she watched him closely for some sign. His face was deeply tanned, he had long curly eyelashes, and a soft voice. There were lines across his forehead and they cut into the corners of his eyes. His black hair turned back in fine waves. He was a quiet and gentle man—not boisterous or noisy. Maybe he was trying to keep his strange behavior under control. Clare became afraid of talking to him. Afraid he might start to tell her

about his pursuit of other men. Or that he would go into a rage or
start to cry—if he was "off," anything was possible. She kept her distance. When he went to kiss her, she turned away; when he offered
her five shillings to buy herself a treat, she said "no, thank-you." She
spoke to him only when he spoke to her—and then her answers were
brief and to the point. And she hoped he asked her nothing else. She
did not know why her fear of him was so strong—only that Boy
spoke of his cousin with a certain pitying tone; Dorothy had said he
was hopelessly afflicted; and the family talked of how there was no
room for such people in Jamaica. It must have been caused by inbreed-
ing. Or the English residents and American tourists—they brought all
manner of evil to Jamaica. How could Robert do this to the family—
Clare heard that question more than once—yet she understood that
he was ill. If he was ill, surely he was not to blame? But it seemed that
this was one illness for which the victim was liable. Sufferers of this
malady could ruin entire families. "A spoiled man. A spoiled man,
I tell you. His mother did not wean him soon enough," one older
relation—a doctor—stated. So now the disease was the fault of
Robert's mother. Clare was too young, perhaps, and too much under
the influence of family gatherings and whispers to ask the question they
all begged: What was wrong with lying down beside another man?

   She tried to put her uncle and his illness from her mind. And finally Robert did what Clare understood many "funny" "queer" "off"
people did: He swam too far out into Kingston Harbor and could not
swim back. He drowned just as Clinton—about whom there had
been similar whispers—had drowned. The stigma was removed, the
family became more relaxed, telling each other there had been an un-
commonly strong riptide that afternoon.

   Now Clare herself had a dearest friend who was dark, but
it would not have occurred to her to place those swift and strong
feelings—largely unspoken feelings—she had for Zoe in the category
of "funny" or "off" or "queer." (Where had Robert placed his feelings
for his own dearest friend—that she would never know.) They were
girls—not men. And it seemed, or she had heard, that "funny" people
were only battymen. Men like Robert and like Clinton. Men with crazy
or overprotective mothers. And Clare had not really thought about
her feelings for her friend in any specific way—she only felt when she
saw Zoe lying on the rock beside her that she wanted to keep her
there. This seemed—or would have seemed, had she thought about

it—a world removed from bringing an American Negro sailor home to meet her father and mother.

If Clare felt anything was wrong with her feelings about Zoe and her concern about losing Zoe's friendship—that those feelings should be guarded from family, for example—this would have originated in what she had been taught and what she had absorbed about loving someone darker than herself. This was where Robert's experience and hers collided. She had been carefully instructed by her father, primarily, and by others also; about race and color and lightening. She didn't yet know how much she had been influenced by these teachings. He who taught her his concepts and theories about the Jews and Stonehenge and space travel also tutored her about the expectations he had with regard to her pursuit of shade. And warned her against what he thought could become a dangerous concern for the "underdog." He had heard it in her words when she asked him about the Holocaust. She knew, that when the time came, should she choose a husband darker than herself, it would be just as if she were Ivanhoe choosing Rebecca rather than Rowena. Boy would place her family outside—"beyond the pale," he said. He also implied that if she chose a darker husband, others would know that she was sexually impure and forced to make the best of it. What other reason would she possibly have? Boy taught his eldest daughter that she came from his people— white people, he stressed—and he expected Clare to preserve his green eyes and light skin—those things she had been born with. And she had a duty to try to turn the green eyes blue, once and for all— and make the skin, now gold, become pale and subject to visible sunburn. These things she should pursue.

As Boy lectured about color, Kitty said little, counseling only that her eldest daughter "live and let live," and "not hate." Kitty's own actions—her private tears, her trips to distribute food and clothing, her attention to the ancient knowledge, and her belief in the power of this, over which she had placed only the thinnest layer of Christian doctrine, and dealt with this doctrine only when it did not threaten her original beliefs—all these things made it appear—and proved to Clare—that her mother cherished darkness. As Kitty held darkness dear, she avoided intimacy—that is, she held no close relations with anyone but her pretentiously whitish husband. That was the mystery.

Kitty wore her love for Black people—her people—in silence, protecting it from her family, protecting the depth of this love from all but herself. Kitty could have been the Maroon Girl in the poem—poised against the curiosity of all lighter than herself and her people. Although she was in fact quite light-skinned, the shade of her younger daughter, like the inside of a Bombay mango when the outside covering is cut away. But color is of course often metaphorical, and Kitty judged her shade with an inner eye. She poised herself against the attacks of the colonialists which threatened her people, her island. Kitty should have been the daughter of Inez and Mma Alli, and Nanny too—and had she known of the existence of these women, she might have shared her knowledge, her extraordinary passion, using its strength, rather than protecting what she felt was its fragility. The fragility of her people, on this island intent on erasing the past. Perhaps her marriage to Boy was an attempt to contain colonialism in her own home—not conscious, of course. Both Boy and Kitty were locked in the past—separate pasts to be sure, but each clung to something back there. For Boy it was Cambridge University and sugar plantations and a lost fortune. For Kitty it was what had been done to her people when they were slaves.

Kitty's mistake in all of this was casting her people in the position of victim, so that her love of darkness became a love conceived in grief—a love of necessity kept to herself. The revolution had been lost when the first slave ships arrived from the west coast of Africa, and she felt Black people were destined to labor under the oppression of whiteness, longing for a better day but not equipped, Kitty believed, to precipitate the coming of the better day. Looking into the past their history could be kept alive on tongues, through speech and in songs—but too much of their future lay at the bottom of the sea in lead coffins or scattered through the earth on the plantations. For all its tenderness, her vision was sad.

If Kitty could have shared her love-which-proceeded-from-darkness with anyone, it would have been with Jennie, her younger, darker child, in the same position at birth as Kitty herself. Maybe someday her breech-born youngest daughter would be admitted into that place deep in Kitty's soul which she kept guard over. But Clare would never gain admission—she had been handed over to Boy the day she was born—swiftly, with the water, surrounded by a caul. And much too soon. The occasional trips Clare took with Kitty into the bush were burned into the girl's memory—they were among the best memories she would ever have, even if she lived to be a hundred. But the trips always stopped short, interrupted by the roar of the river, a sudden storm, an invasion by an army of biting ants, so tiny you didn't know they were there until they attacked. What would happen when Jennie became the one old enough to travel through the bush and across the riverrocks with her mother.

Maybe Kitty never questioned this decision of hers to keep darkness locked inside. Perhaps she assumed that a light-skinned child was by common law, or traditional practice, the child of the whitest parent. This parent would pass this light-skinned daughter on to a white husband, so she would have lighter and lighter babies—this, after all, was how genetics was supposed to work, moving toward the preservation of whiteness and the obliteration of darkness. A white man's science for true. Better to have this daughter accept her destiny and not give her any false notion of alliance which she would not be able to honor. Let her passage into that otherworld be as painless as possible. Maybe Kitty thought that Clare would only want this thing, to pass into whiteness, looking as she did, speaking well because of her lessons at St. Catherine's, reading English books and English descriptions of history. Perhaps she thought it would be best for her.

The only thing English that Kitty remembered from Mr. Powell's school was that silly poem "Daffodils," about a flower she had never seen, which he had made them learn by heart, and one of the children had colored a deep red—like a hibiscus. The red of a flame. Kitty had been the Maroon Girl at the school in her thirteenth year, and *that* was the poem she had taken to heart.

Kitty's quiet, in her marriage and motherhood such a part of her personality, had not always been with her. Before she met Boy, she had been known as a girl eager to get ahead, to get herself an education, and she scoffed at marriage. She was determined to become a schoolteacher and to build her own school in St. Elizabeth, where she would teach children not from the manuals sent by the colonial office, but from manuals she herself would write. This was a grand dream, but she believed she could do it. She had been touched by Mr. Powell's teachings of Black poetry and Jamaican landscape. It seemed to her both logical and possible to build a school on a piece of land Miss Mattie would give her, and teach country children about their own island, while pretending to adhere to the teachings of the Crown. She would go beyond Mr. Powell in her lessons—that was her plan. Instead the war came, and she enlisted as a secretary in a branch of the colonial service, then was transferred to the consulate in Washington, D.C. She needed to get her papers to begin teaching as soon as the war was over, and thought that if she proved herself a worthy subject, then her papers would come all the sooner.

But on her return she met Boy. Then came an evening at Hope—the Royal Botanical Gardens. They were at the center of the maze. A peacock interrupted them briefly with his rough screech—but there was no stopping Boy. And then she married him—much too fast, most people said. Her mother had tried to stop the marriage, convinced that Boy was an inheritor of bad traits and a liking for rum. Clare was born the January after the marriage, and Kitty's life was locked into place.

People said she had been so serious about her dream. But that it was, after all, only a dream, and a good-looking girl like Kitty was better off married anyway. She still thought about her thatched-roof school with the open sides, so the children wouldn't get hot and so they could see the beauty of the country around them. Kitty's choice of land to build on was a flat and sheltered quarter-acre, just past Granny's coffee piece; she had passed through it several times with Clare, but had mentioned it only once.

"How come you didn't do it, Mother?"

"Because I met your father."

"Why couldn't you do it when you were married?"

"You know how your father hates the country," she snapped at her daughter, as though Clare knew something she did not know and was being perverse in her questioning.

"Boy only wants to live in a city. You're lucky we're still in Jamaica, he's always nagging me to move to New York. It's only money stopping him. Heaven help us if he wins big at Caymanas."

"Tell me about the school," Clare asked, wanting to know how her mother's life might have been without her.

"Nothing to tell. It never happened. Let's go find some coconut and ask Joshua to crack it for us."

"Do you think you'll ever build your school?"

"Only if I outlive your father; and that I doubt." She gave a slight little laugh and turned away from her daughter, moving through the bushes and toward her own mother's house.

Kitty usually ignored Boy's pretensions about whiteness and lightness, giving him room for his delusions. Rarely did she flash with anger. Once, when the family was driving through one of the shanty-towns of Kingston—on an unavoidable detour—they saw a dark woman squatting to pee in the gutter. Boy pointed this out to the family—"What are we to do with people like that." It was a statement, not a question.

"Where you get this 'we' stuff, white man?" Kitty at first masking her anger in a feeble joke.

When Boy responded with, "Come on, Kitty, no matter what you do with them, they'll never be like us," her daughter saw her mother's anger flash without camouflage. "Why don't you shut your filthy hateful mouth, you damn cuffy. She's probably pregnant and alone—something *you* would not know about." Then Kitty had him pull the car over so she could give the woman a few shillings—all that she had in her purse. They drove on in silence until they got home. It was silence that was Kitty's finest weapon—honed carefully over the years of her marriage.

In her love for Zoe, Clare knew that there was something of her need for her mother. But it felt intangible and impossible to grasp hold of.

Chapter Seventeen

Clare and Zoe were trudging toward Miss Mattie's hill. They had left Old Joe at the riverbank covered with flies. The two John Crows had already dug into his belly and were pulling the entrails from his carcass. In a very short time the meat began to smell high, and the girls stopped trying to swat the flies away and partly covered Old Joe with palm fronds, giving room to the vultures, who also, it was said, liked to feast on the flesh of living children. The vultures were huge, their dark feathers shiny black against the chestnut brown of the bull. There in the hot sun on a riverbank caked with snot and brain and clotted with blood, the two girls abandoned Old Joe. Clare felt an emptiness low in her stomach—she had killed him. This was not a ceremony she had intended.

Zoe only said that it had been an accident—that Clare was not to blame herself. But in her mind, Zoe was not so much concerned about what would happen to her friend, but that *she* would be blamed somehow for the death of Miss Mattie's bull, and her mother and her sister and herself would have to find another piece of ground to squat on—because Miss Ruthie could never afford to repay Miss Mattie for the death of Old Joe. Clare had pulled the trigger, oh yes, and had sounded off like *buckra* when she should have kept still—the man would have gone off for sure—but everyone who heard it would say that Zoe should have stopped her. Lord, have mercy, wunna never shoot gun into bush—the gal could have hit smaddy. Anybody. How could she let a *buckra* town gal lead her into this? The talk would turn on her for sure—and soon she would be the "pickney what kill Miss Mattie bull."

She had tried to stop Clare—on the hill she managed to get her to give up the hunt for the wild pig. She had tried to tell her what the real consequences of killing would be. For a *buckra* girl and a dark girl. She wondered how much her friend had heard of her words. But they most likely wouldn't have caught the pig anyway. Even if they had seen him, and he, them, him no would have run back a bush—to him lair? Poor Old Joe must have run like the devil when he heard the shot. Only to reach the end of his rope. She should have kept her mouth shut tight and let Clare slash away in the heat at the old trees and vines until she tired herself out and gave up of her own accord. She should have kept her fingers tight around Clare's wrist, and not have let her brush them away. Why hadn't she?

In her mind she could see her mother dismantling the thatch and packing up the bed and the cot and their cooking utensils and begging Mas Freddie a ride in LIGHTNING to find another place to live. And it would all be her fault—all because she had gotten too close to a *buckra* girl and had not kept to her distance and her own place.

"Zoe, wunna better go home now," Clare interrupted her friend's thoughts at the foot of Miss Mattie's hill, still out of sight of the porch. "Me no want Grandma to know dat wunna was with me in this."

"Okay, man; walk safe." Zoe knew that this was a goodbye—and she hoped that Clare would stick to her word and not mention her name. Clare did not know that this was a goodbye—that was another piece of difference that came between them.

~⁀

As with any child who has done a terrible thing, Clare was frightened to face her elders—in this case her grandmother. To tell the long story of what had happened. To wait for punishment while her grandmother traced her character. She held in herself two distinct fears—and the one she felt at the river was different than the one she felt now. It was as if the worst had already happened. Walking up the hill she decided to tell Miss Mattie as little as possible, and to leave out Zoe's name unless she was asked directly about her friend. Then she would deny that Zoe had any part in the morning. And she would face up to Miss Mattie and lie brazenly if her grandmother pressed her. She could say that Zoe had been sick that morning and had gone back home. It was what she needed to do. If she mentioned Zoe's name at all, Miss Mattie would forbid her to ever see Zoe again. That she knew, and that was what made her decide to lie. She never thought that Zoe was in any real danger.

Walking up that hill, she tried to make her face as sad as she could without actually crying. The rifle slapped her side as she walked, and the metal barrel, heated in the sun, burned her thigh. She needed to make the weapon as inconspicuous as possible, and so put it behind her, now walking with her hands at her back. She saw Miss Mattie on the porch—sitting there with a cup of coffee in her hand, face blank and patient—and Clare was unable to make contact with her grandmother's eyes, even though she was only thirty yards away. Miss Mattie had heard the report of the gun, twice, which echoed off the riverwater and the rocks and traveled up the hill to her house. She had heard the wild bellows of Old Joe in between the shots. She had seen the John Crows circle and then disappear beneath the coconut palms that marked the course of the river and blocked the view from her porch. She was a keen-eyed woman who missed little. At first she didn't think her granddaughter was anywhere to blame for those signs. But then the cane-cutter had come running up her hill and had given her the news. "Miss Mattie, wunna grandchild shoot Old Joe. Me no have no part inna it." That was all he said to her, and she had nodded at him and gone inside to check the gun cabinet.

Clare approached the porch and walked to the edge, but did not go up the steps. From there, her eyes level with the rolls of cotton stocking beneath her grandmother's knees, she told Miss Mattie about Old Joe, never once raising her eyes, only concentrating on the folds of flowered hem slightly above the rolls of beige cloth. After she had finished her brief description of half-truth, half-lie, Miss Mattie spoke to her. In a soft voice.

"What was wunna t'inking of, eh? To tek de gun fe wunna uncle to river? Wunna say wunna plan fe shoot bird. Me no believe wunna. Wunna no say wunna is gal pickney? Me no want wunna to stay wit' me no more. A-tall, a-tall. Wunna will have to remove wunnaself to Kingston, to wunna mother and father. Me no want wunna around here. Me no want to look pon wunna. Wunna is a wicked, wicked gal. Wunna will be punished by God fe dis. Me no need fe punish wunna."

Miss Mattie stopped, sighed deeply, then looked toward her flower garden and continued.

"Is Zoe put wunna up to dis, nuh?"

"No, Grandma; it was my idea. Zoe felt sick and went home." Again, Clare dropped her patois. Perhaps judging the distance between them as now unbridgeable.

"Den wunna should not be her friend. Wunna is too mean. Me gwan fe tell Zoe mother dat she not to see wunna anymore, a-tall, a-tall."

And she of course had this power—just as she had been able to begin the friendship between the two girls, now she could end it. Just like that. On and on she went. Moving now from the second to the third person—as if declaiming about her granddaughter to a judge or jury—or God. About the child's wickedness. How this wickedness must come from the girl's father's family. Misbegotten people and a misbegotten girl. The Savages were known all over Jamaica for their devilish ways. Their corruption. She had not wanted her daughter to marry a Savage. And this was the result of that hurried marriage: A beautiful pickney who was mean inside. No good, a-tall, a-tall. A girl who seemed to think she was a boy. Or white. She would surely end up at the Alms House in Black River or worse with her ways.

Miss Mattie sat down that afternoon and wrote a letter to her daughter, telling her to come and get Clare, and said further that Clare was no longer welcome in her house. She was a godless child. She had taken—stolen—a gun and killed Miss Mattie's best animal out of sheer spitefulness.

All Clare told her grandmother was that she had taken the gun to shoot birds "for dinner" by the river and had shot Old Joe by accident. She didn't tell her anything about the pig or the cane-cutter—or that she and Zoe had been naked on the rocks.

~~~~~

As the years had gone by, Miss Mattie had become closer to her Black father, Samuel, and removed from her white mother, Judith. After the death of Miss Judith, Mas Samuel came to live with Miss Mattie and her husband. Miss Mattie's love for her father and her love for her church ruled her existence. When Mas Samuel passed on, her devotion to the church expanded into the space which was left. Miss Mattie practiced her religion every livelong day of her life. She wore long cotton print dresses, which she sewed herself, even in the hottest weather, only turning up her wrist-length sleeves to work in her flower garden by the graves. On her legs were heavy lisle stockings; on her feet, tied-up black leather shoes. That was her everyday costume. On Sundays, and at Wednesday evening meeting, she wore a dress of heavy black taffeta, dark stockings and dark shiny "good" shoes, and a black straw wide-brimmed hat on her head. On those days when her parlor became the house of God, she kept her hat fast on her head, even as she cooked dinner following meeting.

~~~~~

Kitty is a child of four. This is her first memory. Her mother and sister and her brothers are seated around the dining table, waiting for their father, Mas Albert, to return from Kingston with the money he had gotten from selling the crop of sugar cane he and his sons had cut. It is around 1932. Kitty remembers waiting until late in the night for her father—being passed from lap to lap, her brother's-shirt-now-her-dress getting rumpled and tangled in her journey around the dining table. She remembers finally falling asleep.

The Freemans were poor—growing some cane on a few acres to sell, growing food and coffee on the others for the family and people around them. On the land that was left was their four-room house and an old cow tied in the yard—and some chickens wandering about, scratching here and there, and sleeping in the shade trees of the coffee piece. Miss Judith's coffee. Miss Mattie used all the land in those days; Mas Albert would not hear of lending out an acre. She would have to wait until he got senile or died.

The family bathed in the river. Early each Sunday morning before meeting. The water was cold-cold, as cold as the ice delivered every other week. First, the boys bathed with their father. After the boys returned they passed the piece of soap on to their sisters and the girls left with their mother for Annie's Hole. The girls and their mother bathed in thin cotton slips and the girls only detected the bare outline of their mother's body when the riverwater soaked through her garment.

There was no toilet in the small house; chamber pots were used at night, the outhouse in the daytime. A dark and foul-smelling cubicle furnished with a wooden seat which was suspended over a hand-dug pit about ten feet deep. There were torn newspapers piled in a corner. And a family of poly lizards made their home there. Kitty and her sister thought them filthy to live in such a place. The lizards moved fast, running through the newspaper and skating down the walls. They could turn from green to black to red to orange whenever they pleased, it seemed; or could keep their bodies green while passing their tails through the spectrum of color. Sometimes, when one of the girls was seated over the open hole in the middle of the wooden bench, a lizard fell from the ceiling, its claws extending in fear and becoming entangled in her braids—then, no matter how loud she screamed, the lizard remained there, until someone removed each claw from where it grasped the strands, or scalp. For hours afterward the sensation of the lizard's claws stayed with the victim.

The night of Kitty's first memory the family sat around the old dining table which Mas Samuel had built from some mahoe wood he begged someone. The children thought about the money their father would bring back from town and what the family would do with it. And they thought about the presents he had promised them. The girls played with dolls their brothers carved from thread spools dis-carded by Miss Mattie. The boys made their own cricket bats from co-conut stalks and cricket balls from bamboo roots. They made cars with wheels of old shoe-polish tins. And played marbles with the black seeds of the ackee. A real toy—store-bought—was something none of them had ever known. That night, lit by a kerosene lamp at its lowest glare, to save the wick and the fuel, the children moved from sleep to consciousness and back again, and talked about their father and what he might bring them. Miss Mattie said not a word.

She didn't speak when she heard his horse ride up. Nor when he staggered through the back door of the house and into the dining room, with a crumpled brown paper bag in one hand and his riding whip in the other. He smelled high of rum. He said he had been rid-ing all night. That he had been delayed in Kingston and that the mar-ket was bad for sugar cane, so he had only a few shillings to give his wife. But, he said, as the family watched him, his eyes unfocused and half-shut, he had brought the children some hot cross buns—it was Easter time, and they were an old tradition. He threw the paper bag on the table and staggered off into the darkness of the parlor, where he passed out in a wooden chair in a corner. The children waited as the eldest son opened the sack and began to distribute the buns their father had brought them all the way from Kingston. The bag was stained on the outside, but they paid no mind; they had been waiting all night for this. The hot cross buns—which Miss Mattie did not ap-prove of, thinking that they made light of the crucifixion, were mixed in the sack with pieces of horse manure. Kitty whimpered softly and then fell asleep.

Their father's horse had stumbled on the clay road and he had re-trieved the buns in the darkness and in his drunkenness.

Years afterward, whenever the Freemans got together, some one of them would tell the story of that night—as if it was a family joke.

Over the years Miss Mattie spoke less and less to her husband. Now that he was senile and incontinent much of the time, she took care of him as a wife is supposed to, and waited for him to die. But she rarely spoke directly to him. She fed them, emptied his chamber pot when he used it, cleaned the floor around it when he missed the mark, scrubbed his clothes, and washed his body—but she rarely spoke. She had converted him to her faith a few years before, because she wanted to do what she could to save his soul. When she kept church, she seated him on a wooden chair in a corner of the parlor, but it was she who led the service and he only sat there with a faint smile on his face, as if remembering his earlier days, while the others, the righteous ones, talked of retribution and forgiveness, pride and sloth, and the vision of Paul on the Road to Damascus. Mas Albert was beyond praying for his own redemption—his wife and her con-gregation did that for him.

When his outside children came to visit him, Miss Mattie wel-comed them and gave them tea, but she left them alone with their fa-ther and she never asked after their mothers.

Miss Mattie was known all around St. Elizabeth for her goodness. In her life she had taken in the children of other women as her own grew, and Kitty's memories included her mother's adoptions, who came into the house and shared her pallet, and whom she took with her to Mr. Powell's school and looked after them. Miss Mattie shared her home with homeless children and shared her family's food with people who had nothing but the enamel cups and bowls—their "utensils"—they held up at her back window at meal time. She filled their utensils with yam, cassava, ackee—even chicken, if there was any extra.

Her goodness approached renown. If anyone dared to question it within a sixty-mile radius, that person would be met with a stern challenge from almost anyone—as though they had insulted Massa God himself.

What follows is Kitty's second memory. From the year she was seven. She was taken ill one afternoon at Mr. Powell's school with a throat that burned and hurt and a high fever. Her throat was badly swollen and it was impossible for her to take anything without throwing it up—which, with a swollen throat, was awful in its pain. Mr. Powell sent Kitty home that afternoon to Miss Mattie. The pain and burning did not stop and the swelling did not diminish after three days—even with all manner of poultice and liniment applied to the child's throat. Her throat was closing up, and she was burning with fever. Miss Mattie was almost at a loss, when she remembered the district hospital at Black River, and the fact that the traveling surgeon visited there the fifth of every month. This was January third; there was enough time to get Kitty to the surgeon.

Miss Mattie arranged with her neighbor, Miss Esther, to send over her daughter Clarinda to take Kitty to the hospital. Clarinda was a tall, well-built girl, fifteen years old—but not quite right in the head. A little slow. What they used to call dull. People said it was because she had been born with a full set of teeth. Because of the teeth she had bitten her mother's breasts until they bled, and so was never able to receive proper nourishment as a baby. This loss had affected her brain. But Clarinda, whom they called Clary, was the sweetest girl anywhere, and she was faithful to any task assigned her, as long as it was carefully explained. She had never been known to veer from her instructions.

Miss Mattie gave Clary a piece of paper to give to the surgeon, telling what was wrong with Kitty and that he should cut if necessary. She tied both girls on Mas Albert's horse, gave them a parcel of coffee for the parish nurse and an enamel container of broth, and told Clary not to stop for anything and to ride straight through to Black River. Clary was tied in front, Kitty behind her, and it took them the better part of one day to get to the hospital. But they finally made it and settled down to wait for the surgeon's attention.

The district hospital was a low wooden building, pale yellow in color, with only a few rooms off the main waiting room. It looked like someone's shabby old house more than a hospital—but you could tell it was a hospital, or an alms house, or some other official building, by the crowds of people lining the verandah and the steps, trying to get in. The waiting room was packed with poor people, there to have themselves attended to by the surgeon, or by the parish nurse, who was always in residence. The parcel of coffee helped the girls get through the lines, as the people stood back to let them pass, because Clary told them she had an important package for the nurse. But the people also took pity on the two girls, especially the little one with the gray face and the white cloth tied around her neck.

In the corner of the waiting room where Clary spread a towel for Kitty to sit on, she herself standing by her charge, there were several other children—some with deep cuts in need of stitches and tetanus shots, a few with dog bites, one or two with deeply embedded splinters, which no amount of brown soap and wet sugar had been able to budge. A woman—old and feeble-looking—wheezed in a corner. The air was still and close, stirred only by some women with makeshift fans, holding the pieces of cardboard or folded newspaper close to their faces as they waved them slowly back and forth. A few of the fanning women were big-bellied, and talked over their troubles in quiet voices.

A yellow man sat patiently and held a clear glass jar filled with a colorless liquid in front of him. The liquid was bay rum and within it was contained the man's right thumb, which had been chopped off in a canefield the week before. The place where the thumb had been was all healed over by now, but the poor man was right-handed and cane-cutting was his livelihood and he needed the thumb for his work. He could not swing his machete with any power, couldn't even grip it properly, in his present state. He had come to ask the surgeon to sew it back on, and had been keeping it clean for that very reason.

Occasionally a fly landed on the lip of the jar with the thumb and the man wearily waved it away with his four-fingered hand.

The flies were everywhere, even though the atmosphere was heavy with the smell of DDT, sprayed from time to time by the parish nurse with the flit gun she kept always by her side. On the bench right next to Kitty and Clary was a woman who moaned from a terrible pain in her head, and an old man with a piece of bandage trailing from his right ankle. The flit gun made Kitty retch, and she vomited the broth on the floor where it ran across the man's bandage. "Poor little t'ing," the woman sighed. "Poor little t'ing."

Clary sank down on the floor beside Kitty, tried to cover the vomit with the edge of the towel, and put the younger child's head in her lap, rubbing her temples gently and telling her, "sleep, now, sweetie; mus' try to sleep." The nurse finally noticed them, was given the parcel of coffee by Clary, and called over the surgeon. The doctor took Kitty into an examining room, and Clary came too, because, she told them, she had promised Miss Mattie that she would not leave Kitty's side. She watched as the surgeon squeezed the sides of Kitty's throat, and the child screamed weakly with pain. Clary slapped the surgeon's hand away.

"No do dat, Massa! No dare do dat!"

"I have to see what is causing her troubles, gal. If you don't keep yourself quiet I'll have to send you outside."

"Jus' don't hurt her no more."

Clary was quiet after that, but she kept a watchful eye on this big red man with thick spectacles and hands rubbed raw from scrubbing. After a while the red man turned to Clary and told her that Kitty had severe tonsilitis and that he would have to remove her tonsils, because they were distended and filled with poisons, almost cutting off the child's breath. Clary told him she would stay with "de pickney of Miss Mattie," and only then would she let him do the surgery. The surgeon mumbled something under his breath about the "ignorance" of country people, then had the nurse put a mask on Clary's face and place her on a chair alongside a wall of the operating "theater," a room not much larger than Miss Mattie's parlor. After the operation Clary slept on the floor of the ward by Kitty's bed, getting up to see that the horse of Mas Albert was fed and watered, and making herself useful by fetching things for the other patients on the ward. The parish nurse sent word to Miss Mattie that her daughter would be at the hospital for a week or so, and then she would beg her a ride home, because she would not be able to travel on horseback. It took the nurse a long time to convince Clary to ride the horse alone, without Kitty; she only agreed after the nurse showed her the car in which Kitty would travel and swore that she would drive it herself. The nurse washed out the enamel pan and filled it with hot coffee, and Clary rode home by herself.

When the nurse's car got to Miss Mattie's hill, Miss Mattie was at the foot to greet it. She carried her daughter up to the house and into the parlor in her arms, and set her down on the bed she had fixed on the settee. She then thanked the parish nurse for seeing that her daughter got home safe, and gave her an Ovaltine tin filled with roasted cashews.

Kitty remembered everything that had happened to her at the poor people's hospital, except the actual operation. She would remember the thumb-in-the-jar all her life. And she would not forget Clary's devotion—holding her hand night after night, singing to her, jumping up to get her cool water from the well out back. But all through her life Kitty never told a soul about her experiences there. She knew that Miss Mattie had many responsibilities besides her youngest child. She knew that people depended on Miss Mattie. The land depended on her. Her adoptions depended on her. The hungry people who came each day with their empty utensils had need of her mother. And she still wondered about the absence of Miss Mattie and the presence of Clary during those days. Miss Mattie nursed her when she returned home, but neither one, mother or daughter, ever talked about the hospital—not when Kitty was seven, not when she was thirty-five.

Kitty told Boy he could name their eldest daughter after the college his grandfather attended at Cambridge University—when in fact she was naming her first-born after Clary, the simple-minded dark girl who fought for her and refused to leave her side, and was such an important part of her second memory. But Kitty never told this to Clare—that her namesake was a living woman, a part of her mother's life, rather than a group of buildings erected sometime during the Middle Ages for the education of white gentlemen. Clare never knew whom she was called after—whom she honored.

Miss Mattie did not speak about her own childhood to her children—or to many other people for that matter. Had she done so, her children might have been able to understand her better. Awe might have given way to something else. The slaves were freed by the Crown in 1834, and Miss Mattie was not born until 1892, but she knew the kind of slavery which had followed on emancipation. She was sent out by her mother to cut cane when she was ten years old, and worked beside other children and some adults in British-owned fields at a wage never to surpass threepence per day, in a day of twelve hours, in a week of six days.

Her children knew nothing of this experience, or of the beatings she had received at the hands of the overseer for not moving fast enough through the long corridors of cane. Perhaps she had fixed shame to this part of her past. Even she herself tried to forget it. But when she read the Book of Ruth she remembered a little. Ruth the gleaner. Mattie the cane-cutter. Women always working the fields alongside the men. Women with tiny babies, setting them in the sun so their eyes would shut and they would sleep and the women would get some peace. To work. To finish. To delay the next beating. Girl-children working alongside boy-children. Always, it seemed, laboring in some other person's fields. But Miss Mattie had known no kindly Boaz, only landlords which were absentee—Englishmen—delegating their power to the drivers of the gangs. The overseer who had beat her was actually a cousin of hers. He gave no excuses. Just said to work faster, that she was lazy, just like all Jamaicans were lazy. Ruth and Naomi, women left to fend for themselves. All her life Mattie Freeman had fended for herself. Even in marriage.

Her children knew nothing of this experience, except that Miss Mattie would walk for nine miles whenever there was an election, all dressed in her church clothes—nine miles in the heat, wearing a long dress, straw hat, tied-up shoes and lisle stockings, to cast her vote for Alexander Bustamante, whether his name was on the ballot or not. She explained to her children that he was the man who had brought the minimum wage to the workers of Jamaica and for that she would be eternally grateful. She did not mind his reputation as a womanizer, a man who liked to crack the heads of those who disagreed with him—who carried two pearl-handled six-shooters and was rumored not to think twice before using them. She remembered her hours and days and weeks in the canefields, her legs scored and sore and scarred from the razor-sharp thin green blades which grew perpendicular to the woody part of the cane—the source of sugar.

And so she walked to vote for Bustamante—for whom they named a hard flour-and-molasses cake—Bustamante's Backbone. And whom the queen knighted in the late fifties.

Chapter Eighteen

Mrs. Beatrice Phillips was certain of two things in this life: that "colored" people were not to be trusted, and that she had not one drop of the blood, not one stroke of the brush. She had been a girlhood friend of Isabel Savage, who died in an old people's home in New York City in 1949, calling out to a Reverend Sparrow she was sure was perched on the radiator in her room and had been sent to accompany her soul to paradise. Isabel's only son, an insurance agent in Trenton, New Jersey, was not at her side.

Beatrice was not senile and she was not ready to die at all. She was eighty-seven years old in 1958 and had buried each of her thirteen children. They died early of diphtheria and typhoid and malaria; or later of cancer and accident and cirrhosis. In the graveyard at St. Ann's Bay, she had gathered their remains and created a rectangle of graves; the space in the center of the rectangle would be hers, when her time came. She would be in the middle, her angel-babies all around her. Her husband's grave overlooked the rectangle; many years ago she had placed him on a slight rise, about twenty yards from the rest of his family.

Mrs. Phillips blamed Jamaica for the deaths of her children and her curse, or what she felt was her curse—of being a woman who had buried every living thing she had ever loved. People considered her a bitter and miserable woman—a cruel cruel woman—and there was no one left alive to tell them otherwise. Her only living relative was her sister, Mrs. Winifred Stevens, who lived on a piece of Beatrice's property. The two rarely spoke to one another and their relations had always been difficult. The people who worked for Mrs. Phillips excused her bitterness and cruelty by way of her tragedies. Surely the greatest loss a woman can suffer is to bury her own children—was what they said.

Beatrice Phillips passed through the streets of Kingston every day in a chauffeured Packard, black and polished by Edgar, her driver.

Inside the car she sank into the gray wool of the backseat, her cloud of white hair often the only part of her visible through the windows. So that people who did not know her could mistake her for some *buckra*'s pampered poodle on the way to get a trim at one of the pink-and-white hotels. Mrs. Phillips would not have had a poodle—she was a utilitarian, a woman who got value for her money; behind her back people said she pinched a penny until it gave birth to a shilling. A poodle or some such lap dog would be wasteful. Her dogs came from the back alleys of Trench Town, where they had been bred for survival. Mrs. Phillips fed them and fattened them and trained them to watch her house and to attack any Black person who entered the yard. To bark at all those who walked down the street. At the sight of a Black person on the road, the dogs would mass and charge, almost climbing the gate in their frenzy, baring their teeth, growling, often with little white-haired Mrs. Phillips at their center. Her dogs kept this noise up until the passerby went on his or her way—and the dogs remained alert all hours of the day and night. Mrs. Phillips had thirteen dogs in her yard at Thirteen Redfield Road, roaming the small patch of ground, which was dry and brown because dog urine had long since killed any grass. Since the yard was small and there were so many dogs, Mrs. Phillips paid an old Black woman five shillings a week to walk the premises daily and shovel up the dog leavings on the ground. The old woman was terrified of the dogs, although Mrs. Phillips had taught the dogs that the old woman, named Minnie Bogle, was an exception to the rule of attack. But the dogs also observed that Mrs. Phillips herself occasionally beat Minnie between the shoulder blades with a stick, so perhaps they thought her punishment was not their lookout.

⁓

Kitty and Boy came down to St. Elizabeth as soon as they got Miss Mattie's letter, a few days after the incident. Boy immediately upon his arrival swore to Miss Mattie—"as God is my witness"—while stepping onto the porch, that he would pay for the loss of Old Joe, and that Clare would be punished accordingly. Miss Mattie did not believe that he would repay her, believing instead that any extra money he got at any time in his life would go to the Caymanas Racetrack or the Appleton Estate, purveyors of rum. Caymanas was a new racetrack, replacing the one on which Boy's forebears once camped. It was built in the middle of the largest sugar plantation on the south coast—literally carved out of the canefields. The visual background of each horserace was acre upon acre of seven- or eight-foot-high sugar cane, moving and rattling in slow counterpoint to the pace and noise of the thoroughbreds. The smell of the live cane—sweet and heavy—was suspended across the track and through the clubhouse and paddock.

The turn-off for Caymanas was on the Spanish Town Road, right by Tom Cringle's Cotton Tree, a huge silk cotton tree which was a Jamaican landmark, from whose branches human bodies had once swung. It had been a hanging tree, used primarily in the punishment of runaways, who may have fled the same fields which now held the sport of kings. Old Joe would not be paid for, Miss Mattie's loss financially compensated, as long as racing was legal in Jamaica. And that would never happen—the races were the most popular form of entertainment on the island, in which day after day, animals competed against one another, running clockwise around a turf track. Clare often accompanied her father to the track—children were allowed in, and were even allowed to wager. But Boy was impatient with his daughter, because she would only play it safe and bet "place" tickets, instead of plunging all her money on "win." The Savage style of gambling.

Miss Mattie did not believe her son-in-law would reimburse her for the loss of her animal, but she thanked him nonetheless and kept quiet, and made herself glad that she would see the last of her eldest granddaughter for a time. She did not think that this exile might teach Clare a lesson—that her granddaughter might mend her ways once punished by a period of banishment. Miss Mattie had made a judgment—that Clare was only what she appeared to be; not of Miss Mattie at all, but of Boy's side of the family. The child had no sense of country. He should be the one to punish his daughter; the girl was his child after all.

The entire time the two waited for Boy and Kitty to arrive, Miss Mattie drilled her considered opinion into her granddaughter's brain. Sometimes conveying her feelings with a glance, or with a verse from the Bible, softly said, toward no specific direction, perhaps addressed only to herself. Othertimes she made her feelings known with a clear statement, to no one in particular, but always in the presence of her granddaughter—"Lord, have mercy, does anybody hear my trials?" Old Joe was gone forever, due to one pickney's wickedness. One gal pickney who was too mean. Miss Mattie repeated and repeated these conclusions and her congregation followed her lead. When they arrived for Wednesday evening meeting, before Clare's parents came to fetch her, they only looked briefly in the direction of the girl, no one now coming forward to touch her hair and comment on its softness, and then offered Miss Mattie their sympathy on her misfortune—a double misfortune in their minds.

Clare could not talk to Zoe, nor could she seek out Mad Hannah, who in the course of that summer had been sent away. She wrote about all these things in her diary, but it wasn't the same as having someone to talk with—who would say that it had been only an accident and that it hadn't really been her fault—countering Miss Mattie's repetition of blame with one of innocence.

She had bought the diary last March, and these were the first entries in it since writing about the movie and Anne. She wrote about Zoe and about that morning. She wrote about being naked with Zoe and about being frightened. She recorded her fear of the cane-cutter—her fear of his seeing her privates—her fear of what she had done. She wrote of missing Zoe. Of not wanting to be selfish. The diary still didn't have a name, and she thought about calling it after her friend—but waited on that, not sure about it.

She thought about feeling lonely. Perhaps loneliness was the thing that made Anne Frank keep a diary in the first place, Clare thought. Was it loneliness that made people write things down? Because she had not felt the need to describe how she felt before this—now as she hid from Miss Mattie's stares, avoiding her grandmother as much as possible, and trying hard to believe that she herself was not truly mean, not damaged in some terrible way. Now that she had no company and had been thrown back into the quiet of the country where the expected noises closed around her. She didn't think she was mean but she believed she was wrong in what she had done. She believed she didn't deserve Anne Frank as a heroine any longer—Anne had never killed anything, had herself been killed. What did Anne know of guns—except those which had been pointed at her. It seemed to Clare that she had switched to the other side without meaning to. And yet there was still a part of her which spoke now and then, telling her that she had not been deliberately cruel, had had a right to the weapon. But this voice was becoming indistinct.

As a child she had to rely on statements from the grown-up outside world about her guilt and her innocence—her character. She was not equipped to judge herself. Nor to connect her act to the defense-lessness of a girl like Anne Frank and other girls she had heard of or known.

She had no choice but to take whatever her judges gave her.

She so wanted to say goodbye to Zoe, but was not allowed by ei-ther parent or Miss Mattie to go over to Breezy Hill and see her friend. The "okay man; walk safe" was the goodbye which would pass be-tween them, which Clare would hold on to, but it was not enough. She wanted to explain her banishment to Zoe. And to tell her that she would write her from Kingston. She could only send word of this by way of Joshua, and he did it for her because she threatened to tell Miss Mattie about the boys eating the hog's privates. It was doubtful that Miss Mattie would have paid any attention to information com-ing from Clare at this moment, but in his position Joshua couldn't take any chances. Clare was still light, and her hair was still soft, and his mother was still a maid to *buckra* people in Kingston. But Joshua said Zoe was not there—unless he had lied.

After their arrival in St. Elizabeth, Kitty and Boy hardly spoke to their daughter. Not directly. Not as if they knew her. Only words of "how could you do this to us" and "your grandmother will never for-give you" and "what are we to do with you" surrounded Clare in the backseat of the car as they drove east—through Old Harbour, where women sold fried fish and cassava cakes at the roadside; past the fields of agave outside Kettle Spring; the herds of white hump-backed Brahmin bulls and their flocks of handmaidens, the tickbirds, near the Rio Cobre, which was red and low; the cotton tree by the race-track entrance; and the small houses of the fieldhands on the Cay-manas Estate—down she sank in the back on the way to Kingston, trying to imagine herself out of the car and into the landscape that passed beside her. These words of her mother and father mixed with other dead-ended statements about what she had done. What they felt about what she had done. Boy said it signified a "point of no re-turn." That frightened Clare almost more than anything else.

Neither parent asked her anything. Not why she had done it. Not how she felt. Whether it was really an accident. No one said that she might have been hurt. They merely chanted their disappointment at her, taking up Miss Mattie's litany and speaking it at their daughter in their own words. Clare had heard herself referred to in the third person so often by now, she almost began to think that they were talk-ing about someone else. Some girl in a story who came to no good.

"This is too serious a business for us just to punish her," Boy's voice concluded.

Something else was on her mind. The night before they left St. Elizabeth she had heard her mother and grandmother talking low in the kitchen. She heard something that would stay with her, although she didn't quite understand it. "You know, Kitty," Miss Mattie said. "You know, you should never have married that man in the first place. Buckra man is jus' no good a-tall, a-tall. De pickney no mus' tek on de blood." Kitty said nothing at first, and Clare was sitting beneath the window in the darkness, not where she would have seen her mother's face. Then she heard her mother whisper, "What choice did I have?"

Boy had been interrupted in the midst of his weekly route for the liquor importers. And Kitty had to take time off from her hotel desk. They seemed in a hurry to get their daughter back to Kingston, and to decide where to put her for the few weeks left of her vacation. They said they were certain she could not stay at home with Dorothy for the rest of the time. They did not tell Clare why. Only that what she had done had to be commemorated in a way that she would not forget— some way had to be found to bring her back to where they thought she was. Her sister Jennie was staying with an aunt, an old great-aunt, across the island in Port Maria, but there would be no room for Clare in her small house—especially when the aunt found out why Clare had been exiled from St. Elizabeth by Miss Mattie.

So, on their return, Boy telephoned Mrs. Phillips, the old Savage family friend, and asked her if his eldest daughter would be welcome in her home for the rest of the school vacation. And during the conversation, from the back of his mind, came, by the way, since her house was within walking distance to St. Catherine's, perhaps Mrs. Phillips would like to keep Clare for part of the school year. She would probably enjoy the company, he said, and Miss Beatrice responded that, yes, she most likely would, since she was getting on and was alone except for her dogs. Oh yes, Boy agreed, that was something to think about, passing lightly over her loneliness and getting on with the purpose of the call. You know, Miss Bea, the girl is getting too old to be traveling on public buses all around Kingston—God knows what might happen to her. Surely you understand. Yes, of course, Miss Bea understood perfectly. Perfectly. Bring the child here.

This decision came about so fast. But both mother and father seemed to think that something appropriate had been done. They relaxed, and spoke to their daughter almost as if nothing had happened.

Boy had handled all the details, but Kitty complied with the decision totally. Or so it seemed. In their conversations together, the pair spoke of how killing the bull was not so much evidence of their daughter's "meanness," but that she was showing signs of something which had to be stopped—corrected—something which might make her wrong-headed. In fact, neither of them talked about the actual slaughter of Old Joe, but about Clare taking the gun and ammunition and sneaking away in the morning without permission. "If she's like this now, what will she become?" Boy asked.

Maybe Kitty thought it was whiteness—and the arrogance which usually accompanied that state—which had finally showed through her daughter's soul. But should she save her daughter from this—or give in to it?

Maybe Boy thought that Blackness was the cause of his daughter's actions—and the irresponsibility he felt imbued *those* people—and now had to be expunged once and for all. On this little island so far removed from the mother country, a white girl could so easily become trash.

But it is doubtful that either parent thought the thing, the "crisis," through with any thoroughness. They said to each other that they had too many problems of their own to now be saddled with what the Americans called a problem child. They had done nothing, they said, to deserve this. They were confused. Other people sent children away to school to learn rules and laws. They couldn't afford a boarding-school, so Mrs. Phillips would have to do.

Clare had been so *quiet*, so girlish, so "demure," her father said, and except for her strangely sympathetic interest in the Jews—which had passed after he spoke to her—she had been until now an exemplary child, an intelligent child. A reader. A winner of prizes. A girl who could recite all the monarchs of England in consecutive order when she was ten years old. She had been no trouble until now.

What did Kitty think? That the thing had to be stopped here. That Clare could go to a university and take on a profession. That Clare would most likely marry a white man and move into a life which would make life easier. And everything the girl had done until now seemed to prepare her for that future.

The images they had of their daughter collided with who their daughter was at this specific time in her life. They were unable to recognize the simplicity of her actions. They were held by the same system her actions encompassed. All she was in those actions escaped them—except the obvious. A girl of twelve was feeling her way into something. A girl of twelve thought that by taking a gun she acquired some power, some independence. She thought she was defending herself and her friend from the stares and shouts of a cane-cutter, and proving she could survive in the bush. Her act—taking the gun and cartridges and setting out in the early morning to hunt—could be seen as poignant. Her act—firing over the head of a man she accused of trespassing—could be seen as arrogant, while at the same time fright just as much as privilege made her fire.

Would Boy and Kitty have thought differently had they known her original target had been a wild pig? Yes—but it wouldn't have worked in the girl's favor. She had stepped out of line, no matter what, in a society in which the lines were unerringly drawn. She had been caught in rebellion. She was a girl. No one was impressed with her.

Mother and daughter were packing Clare's grip, filling it with new school uniforms and clean white blouses.

"But Mother, I don't understand why I have to go live with Mrs. Phillips. I don't even know her."

"Mrs. Phillips has been very kind to take you in." Kitty answered her daughter.

"But why do you have to send me away? Why can't I stay here? I'll be good. I promise. I didn't mean to do what I did. Honest."

"You meant to take the gun didn't you?"

"Yes, but . . ."

"Child, what you did was a very serious thing. Your father is right. Punishment is not punishment enough. You have to learn once and for all just who you are in this world. Mrs. Phillips is a lady, and you are getting to the age when you will need to be a lady as well. She is from one of the oldest families in Jamaica. She has a good education. Good manners."

"But I don't want to be a lady."

"What do you know what you want? Anyway, want has nothing to do with it. Look here, you have a chance someday to leave Jamaica behind you. When you are grown you can want anything you want. You can be anything you want to be. A doctor. A teacher. But to get there you have to learn the rules. That girls like you don't fire guns. Girls like you have a better chance at life than other girls. I know what I am talking about. What I would have given to have the chances you are going to have. Mrs. Phillips can teach you to take advantage of who you are. I can't do that for you."

"I don't understand. You're my mother."

"Jamaica is just a tiny little place. There are no opportunities for someone like you here. I don't want to leave Jamaica because my place is here. But you don't have to be confined by this sad little island. Just take your medicine. Go stay with the old lady and learn what you can from her."

"Is she a nice lady?"

"She seems to be." Kitty paused. "I have only spoken with her once or twice myself. But your father says she is a decent woman—a God-fearing woman. Although I think she is a little old-fashioned."

"Old-fashioned about what?"

"Just a little behind the times, that's all."

"You mean she doesn't have electricity or running water?"

"No, child, she is a rich woman; she has all those things."

"Then how?"

"Well, she is narrow-minded about colored people. You know, a little like your father."

"Then what do you want me to learn from her?"

"I said she would teach you things you could use to better yourself. You will just have to overlook that other part. There are many many narrow-minded people in this world. You have to learn to live among them."

"When will you send for me?"

"In a little bit."

"When?"

"I'm not sure. Your father and I will decide."

"I don't want to go."

"I know. But it's for your own good, you know."

⁓

The Morris Minor drove up to the gate of the home of Mrs. Phillips and one light was visible on the verandah.

"Who is dere, please?" Miss Minnie Bogle shouted over the incredible noise of the thirteen dogs.

"Mr. Boy Savage."

"Jus' a moment, sah. Mek me open de gate."

They drove through the gate and into the dried-up yard, and Boy lifted Clare's grip from the boot of the car. Mrs. Phillips appeared in the doorway—an ancient and whitened lady leaning on a cane of lignum vitae.

Chapter Nineteen

Minnie Bogle moved through the darkness at the side of the house and disappeared around back. She was on her way to the kitchen to tell Hazel, the housemaid, and Elijah, the houseman, that Mr. Savage's daughter had arrived.

"De pickney-of-de-big-buckra-man wha' fe stay wid de ole bitch come," Minnie said.

"Lord, Minnie, no call she 'bitch' in here; suppose she hear wunna? Wunna know say how mean she be."

"Chuh, Elijah-man, what wunna want me fe call she? She no is bitch—surrounding sheself wid dogs fe mess wid she?"

"Minnie! Lord have mercy, you terrible, missis . . ." Elijah turned back to his chopping, and Hazel, glancing in the direction of the old Black lady, sucked her teeth softly, pretending to disapprove of Minnie's talk. Both depended on Minnie to speak about Miss Beatrice as they themselves were not able to. It was an old ritual between the three. Minnie often went into a rant for all their benefit about the "ole bitch" and what she imagined went on in the bedroom after the lights were put out and their mistress brought in two or three or four of her favorite dogs to sleep with her.

Lord have mercy, indeed—those damn dogs ate better than the people standing in the kitchen. Miss Beatrice called them her praetorian guard and she took special care of them. Grooming them herself. Seeing to their insect bites and sores. Even carrying some of them in the back of the Packard when she visited her other properties across the island.

Minnie went on to her comrades—"Den if she no rut wid dem, she no mus' tek dem as she pickney. De lord tek away she true pickney and leave she wid dog. De mother of Satan was one jackal. No forget dat." The others said nothing. Used by now to Minnie and her belief in Miss Bea's meanness. That a woman of such meanness would be capable of anything. Minnie sometimes talked of her mistress in a loud voice at the back of the house, as if she were daring Miss Beatrice to catch her—although she knew full well that after a certain hour the old white lady removed her hearing aid, and so would not detect Minnie's rage.

When Minnie opened the gate for the black body of the Packard to pass through, and each time cast her eyes in a furious beam at the white woman in the backseat, Miss Bea did not notice anything except that the gate was open and the car moved forward. She might also notice that Minnie Bogle was slower than she thought she should have been—probably coming from the kitchen where she was stealing food or getting in the way of Hazel and Elijah, Miss Bea concluded. Or Miss Bea might spy a mound of dog excrement from her side window. With that observation she might ready her cane. Or her tongue. Calling the Black woman *wuthless*, telling her that if it happened again she would turn her out. "And then where are you to go, Minnie Bogle? Who else will take you in?"

The furious beam would not register with Miss Bea, the slowness of Minnie Bogle would not be perceived as part of resistance, because Miss Bea did not believe that Black people could become angry with the likes of her. Oh, yes, they were always chopping each other up, scuffling and brawling in the rumshops and on the streets of Kingston, but that was not the same as anger against their "betters." These people were not capable of a just rage. They were lazy. Lackadaisical. They were sullen and thought about little else than their stomachs. And how to fill them by stealing from people closer to whiteness than themselves, and thus closer to the angels. And so the furious beam cast from the eye of the Black woman went as unnoticed as the shouts she made in the night, unheard by the woman who employed her.

But Minnie's rude talk and her glances and her mutterings as she walked to the gate and dodged the strokes of the lignum vitae were her only ways to get something back for the way she was treated. And she deserved to get something back. The story was too old—she needed the money and the roof over her head, she had to endure the punishment. She was past eighty and couldn't find any other kind of work anywhere. She had no property. No people. But her suffering did not have to be silent. Her anger turned silent when it met with Miss Bea, who was insensitive to it, but for Minnie it was alive, and kept her going.

Clare had met Mrs. Phillips only once before this evening, when the white lady came to Dunbarton Crescent to deliver a plum pudding two Christmases past. The pudding was made according to an old family recipe, given to her by Isabel Savage many years ago. She had encased Isabel's pudding in a hard white-sugar sauce which she said she herself had made, and presented it to the family with her best wishes for the season and in the coming year. "And God save the queen," she closed her greetings, as the family settled by the wireless to listen to the annual message of Elizabeth II. "My husband and I wish you all a Happy Christmas and a prosperous New Year."

Clare had not been to Thirteen Redfield Road before this evening, as her father delivered her to this old family friend. This place was to be her home for a time, and she couldn't even see what the house was like because the only light was from a small yellow bulb on the verandah, and Miss Beatrice was explaining at that moment to Boy that the cost of electricity was highway robbery and it was her practice only to light one light in the evening, every evening.

"And it had better be on the verandah; otherwise all manner of people might be tempted to come in."

Clare could tell that the house was old and wooden, with a slightly peaked roof, and a wide latticed verandah, on which a pack of dogs now moved back and forth. It was typical in outline of many of the houses in this part of Kingston, near to Halfway Tree. The older wealthy families had lived here, until they began to move upwards into Barbican and the hills overlooking the harbor—only a few, like Mrs. Phillips, stayed on, as shopkeepers and civil servants and teachers moved in and around them.

Clare hung back a little, waiting until Boy and Mrs. Phillips, whom she had been instructed to call Miss Beatrice, finished their negotiations.

This was to be her "home," and this white woman was to be her "guardian," Boy told her in the car. "And you are to make yourself at home with her. She would want it that way. She said as much to me. And you are to mind what she says."

Clare had stayed in other people's houses before this, but this was different. She had known the people in those houses and the houses themselves. Here was a house she could not see, and she had no idea when she would be sent for.

⁓

"Goodbye, dear; we'll come see you soon." Boy drove away, and Minnie Bogle reappeared to unlatch the front gate. "Drive safe, sah," was spoken at him. "Damned fool-fool cuffy," said under her breath. Minnie shut the gate and moved off.

"Now, young lady," Clare had been standing on the verandah for at least a half-hour, and this was the first time Mrs. Phillips had addressed her. "Now, young lady, let me show you where we sleep in this house." Miss Beatrice lit a kerosene lamp, which she handed to Clare, and instructed her to lead them to the glass doors at the side of the verandah. Clare walked forward, while Miss Bea poured some kerosene in a milk tin and followed her, the tin in her left hand, her stick in her right. The kerosene sloshed around the tin and smelled strong in the night air.

We sleep—that bothered Clare, who thought that if Miss Beatrice was a rich woman—"rotten rich," Minnie Bogle called her—she would have her own bedroom.

The room that they were to share was directly behind the glass doors. It was large and square, the walls against the light cast by the oil lamp a dingy blue, streaked here and there where mosquitoes had been smashed against the plaster and soot from the glass chimney of the lamp had marred the paint. Two beds, hidden by white mosquito netting, were side by side, separated by a small table. The only other furniture was a large mahogany wardrobe and a cumbersome old bureau with mismatched brass pulls. That was all—and the walls were bare of decoration except for a map of England hanging over one bed, inset with a portrait of the queen.

"Now, my dear, you will sleep in that bed. I've had Hazel make it up all fresh for you." Miss Beatrice pointed to the bed without the map. "The bathroom is through that door; and you can put your things in the bottom drawer of the bureau."

"Yes, Miss Beatrice."

Miss Beatrice drew back the mosquito netting from her bed and settled down, placing the tin of kerosene on the table between.

"We have one task to accomplish before we take our rest." Miss Beatrice focused on the table. "Please go to the door and call for

Margaret, Charles, and Elizabeth." Clare did as she was told, and three of the dogs came running through the french doors.

"Over here, Margaret," Miss Beatrice commanded. And Margaret, a skinny black-and-white mongrel, about the size of a small terrier, came and sat between the beds. "Now kindly shut the doors and bolt them." Once the room was closed, Clare could feel a tickling in her throat, as if she had swallowed a handful of the dogs' fur. The room quickly became hot, because Mrs. Phillips's house allowed no louvers to let in a breeze. Just glass windows and doors—shut tight against the evening. Clare was uncomfortable—she felt held-in—lonely. Who was this woman and what was she to teach her?

"Now, young lady, I will teach you how to take the ticks out of a dog's skin. Ticks are a terrible curse on dogs, and we must remove them, else the insect will suck all the blood from the animal. You feel with your fingertips through the fur, and then, when you feel something like a carbuncle, a hard boil, put your fingernail underneath and pull it out. Like so." She had pried one of the insects loose from the shoulders of Margaret and held it toward Clare. It was fat and round and a gray color in the dim light of the oil lamp. Mrs. Phillips positioned it under her thumbnail; then there was a faint cracking noise, and the white finger was suddenly covered with blood. "I like to crack them. The damned beasts don't deserve to live. But if you don't want to crack them, just drop them in the kerosene tin and they will die of poisoning." Crack again. More blood, a thick drop falling on the wideboard floor.

"They are a danger to my dogs; that I will not endure."

Clare was not a queasy child, but she was having difficulty facing up to this task—this lesson—in her new home.

After they were finished, she pulled the mosquito netting around her bed, said goodnight to Miss Beatrice, and dreamed about getting her monthlies by the side of Miss Mattie's river and using a piece of coconut husk softened with oil to stanch the flow.

When she woke she did not know where she was.

Chapter Twenty

The days at Redfield Road stretched out in a deadly sameness—each kept according to a strict schedule, as might have been expected. And because there were no chores to be done by either Clare or Miss Beatrice, and everything requiring human labor seemed to be accomplished almost magically, finished silently, the days all had the same texture. There was no difference between them: no day when women gathered to wash, no day when the butcher appeared on the doorstep, no week of gathering coffee to blanch and roast and pound. The country around Miss Mattie's house had been still, but this house in town had a different kind of quiet. There were no surprises at all. And there was no playmate to break the silence apart and take Clare into make-believe, where she could pretend she was an Aztec princess kept prisoner by a conquistador. Or a girl whose family had died in a cholera plague, like the girl in *The Secret Garden*, who had managed to find a playmate hidden away.

Miss Mattie had protected Clare from labor, but Miss Beatrice allowed her no movement at all—not even into the kitchen to visit with Hazel or Elijah or Minnie Bogle. Just back and forth between St. Catherine's and the house where all was done for them.

The mornings began with Elijah entering the bedroom with breakfast trays, after announcing himself and his burden in a loud voice. On hearing Elijah's tones, Clare rose and folded back the netting from the two beds—making sure to be well covered by a sheet before Elijah made his entrance, as Miss Beatrice had instructed her. Elijah laid the trays carefully in each lap, did not tarry, and on his exit handed Clare the *Daily Gleaner*. Miss Beatrice fixed her hearing aid to her right ear and pinned the battery to her bosom. Once she was set, Clare began to read from the newspaper: through the headlines, editorials, social notes, to the poems, cartoons, listing of films at the Carib, Rialto, Tropical—even though they did not go to the cinema. Miss Beatrice wanted to know all that was happening around town.

Miss Beatrice was forever talking about "culture" and what a cultural "backwater" Jamaica was. A place whose art was "primitive" and whose music was "raw." But one morning Clare found something in the paper she knew would interest her guardian. Perhaps the two might even attend.

Nestled between the movie announcements and the race results was an article which announced the arrival of the coloratura soprano Lily Pons, to give a concert at the Carib. She was to appear the following week and sing arias from *Lakmé*, *La Sonnambula*, and *The Daughter of the Regiment*. People like Lily Pons hardly ever visited the island, except to take the sun—rarely to perform. Clare read the headline to

Miss Beatrice: "Lily Pons, world-famous coloratura soprano to sing in Kingston . . ."

"What! Read that again."

Clare repeated the words from the newspaper.

"A colored woman! A colored opera singer! What nonsense! Didn't that business with Marian Anderson teach them anything?"

"But, Miss Beatrice . . ." Clare tried to explain what she knew about the opera from the teachers at St. Catherine's. "I think coloratura has to do with the way she sings. It doesn't mean she's colored."

As if she needed to contradict that assumption. As if there was something wrong with being colored. She spoke in earnestness and without thinking and didn't realize the meaning of her defense.

"In my day a colored woman would not have dared. Would not have been allowed . . ." Miss Beatrice was talking over Clare's words—she had not acknowledged the defense.

"Let me see her picture. Is there a picture in the paper? Let me see it." Miss Beatrice was getting angry. And Clare didn't know why the white lady was so angry. But she had become frightened at the depth of what Kitty had called Miss Beatrice's "narrow-mindedness."

"Let me have the paper, I tell you!"

Clare handed the *Gleaner* over to her guardian. In it was a wire-photo of Lily Pons, a little woman with large dark eyes. "Of course she's colored. Look at that face. It gives her away completely. That *must* be what the word means. Don't give me any nonsense, girl. What do you know about it anyway? You're not so pure yourself, you know."

No, Clare thought about herself—she wasn't. But at least she didn't hate.

"Calls herself French, does she? Well, that has always been code for nigger."

Clare looked away from Miss Beatrice—down to her knees, across which she folded her arms.

That was but one incident, and after it Clare learned to keep her mouth shut about anything to do with color or colored people. Anything that might be mistaken by Miss Beatrice for sympathy or concern. She was learning to live with narrow-mindedness. Learning not to wince when the white lady rolled down the Packard window and slid her stick through to slap Minnie Bogle across the shoulder blades. Learning not to smile when she heard Minnie's voice in the kitchen wearing out the "ole bitch."

She spoke to Miss Beatrice only out of politeness, because she was a guest in her house. She waited for Boy and Kitty to come and get her. Not rocking the boat.

Clare was told by Miss Beatrice that they were to travel for a weekend to her house in St. Ann's Bay—the house the white lady had grown up in, where her sister now lived. They traveled together in the back of the Packard, with Margaret and Elizabeth and Charles, Miss Beatrice's favorites, and a hamper packed with tinned sardines and water crackers. They passed across the mountain roads, through villages and beside small cement-block houses, where people came out to look at the huge black car, and children tried to bang on the hood when the Packard slowed. As they rode, Miss Beatrice told Clare about Mrs. Stevens, her elder sister who lived in the house in St. Ann's Bay all the time. Alone, except for her womanservant.

"When we arrive at the house, you are not to go into her part at all. Understand?"

"Yes, Miss Beatrice."

"She is not right in the head and I do not want you talking to her."

"Yes, ma'am."

Miss Beatrice took a sip of green tea from the thermos in her lap. "My sister was too ambitious for herself. Surrounded herself with books. She had some inflated notions about leaving Jamaica. And she did not want to marry—carried on so about that, she nearly killed our father. She finally took to her room, and Father had no choice but to send her to a convent school in Morant Bay."

"Did she become a nun?"

"Good Lord, no. When she got out of school—they dismissed her because they could not control her—when she got out of school, Father had a husband waiting for her, and she was of course made to marry him."

"Oh."

"Now she made the poor man's life a living hell—wouldn't let him come near her at all. So of course he left."

"How come?"

"Couldn't take her selfishness. Just couldn't endure a woman who wouldn't be a woman. You are too young to understand all this anyway."

"Yes, ma'am."

"Then she took it into her head that water was sacred. All water was sacred, and she was not worthy to have it touch her skin. This started when she was going through change-of-life, about thirty-five years ago. Probably felt remorse because she had no babies to keep her in her old age. She stopped washing herself, and hasn't washed since. And now she believes that if water touches her she will die instantly. Lord, she is a crazy old woman."

Clare did not respond. She was thinking about change-of-life, and why so many strange things in women's lives were attached to it. She was not sure what it meant at all—except that it could cause insanity, make women develop paunches or grow beards—bring out the worst in a woman. That was what people said. "She's going through the change." Which explained any bizarre behavior in a middle-aged woman—that is, behavior others judged to be bizarre. Bodies and faces others judged to be ugly or strange.

If a woman had not washed for thirty-five years, what must she be like?

"Anyway, although my sister is mad, she is quite harmless. But she talks all manner of nonsense and will only confuse you. Besides, she is so filthy that you might get a disease from her—herself, she is immune by now. To filth."

"Yes, ma'am."

"And when we get there, be sure to put on your straw hat, with the wide brim; the sun is dreadful on the North Coast. You don't want to freckle."

"No, Miss Beatrice."

The house was set back from the road about fifty yards. Set almost directly against a cascade of water and a wall of rock. It was not unlike the great house at Runaway Bay. The same shape and lowness, same faded wood, same tangled verandah with lizards racing through the vines and woodwork. But this house was lived in, and a plywood wall ran through the length of the house, dividing it exactly in half. On the far side were Mrs. Phillips's country quarters. Pale green walls and narrow beds and a commode under each bed. A ewer and basin on a washstand in a corner of the bedroom. A sitting room arranged with wicker furniture unwinding here and there, and an oriental rug bare of design in places, on the broad-planked mahogany floor. Nothing more than should be there. No books. No magazines. A calendar showing the little princesses during the war.

On the near side of the house, near to where the car was parked, and which Clare and Miss Beatrice had to walk past, all was dimness. Clare glanced to the side to look into Mrs. Stevens's quarters, and could see nothing but a shadow moving back into the depths of the house. Either Mrs. Stevens or Emma, her servant, come to see who had arrived. The shadow disappeared, and the visitors went to their quarters to settle in.

The next morning, early, Clare went out onto the verandah, still wanting to fill out the shadow she had seen yesterday—hoping, of course, that it was Mrs. Stevens and not the woman who worked for her. But this morning she did not have to look far at all, because in the front yard, sprinkling some bread for the birds, was the woman she knew to be Mrs. Stevens. She was unlike any one person Clare had seen in her life—a tall white-haired lady in a ragged blue dress and barefeet. A slender woman with one distinguishing feature, the filth that framed her body. Clare could smell her stench from where she stood—a woman whose skin was flecked and caked with dirt and smelled of urine and sweat and thirty-five years. Her fingernails were long dirty claws. Her white hair spread outward from her head and the spaces on her scalp where her hair had thinned were covered with patches of dirt and scab. The filth was like an aura. Her entire being, it seemed, was unwashed. Clare thought about the leper colony on the island, and imagined that Mrs. Stevens might be a leper. Closed off from human contact by her unwashed being—because lepers were thought to be corrupt. Those who carried bells and called themselves "unclean, unclean."

But Clare was not frightened by Mrs. Stevens. Maybe because she watched her in an act of gentleness—humming to herself as she broadcast the crumbs—and the birds did not turn from her. Maybe because her eyes had now turned to gaze at Clare, and she could see that they were the deepest blue possible. But not cold blue—warm, deep blue, like violets.

"Good morning, Miss Clare." Her voice was calm. What people called "cultured."

"Good morning, Mrs. Stevens."

"Come visit me this afternoon and I'll give you a piece of cake."

"Yes, Mrs. Stevens."

Clare spoke in a low voice, afraid of waking Miss Beatrice and getting caught talking to someone she had been forbidden to seek out. She could not go over that afternoon because Miss Beatrice was around, and had other plans for her, but she went the next day when the white lady left for town to arrange the harvest of her coconut crop. She had been told to stay behind and do her schoolwork.

As the Packard drove off, Clare stepped quietly across the verandah, then called out softly, "Mrs. Stevens, I've come to visit."

"Come in, my dear," a voice called from within the dimness. "No, don't. This place is too untidy. Let me come out and sit with you on the verandah." She emerged from the doorway and Clare saw that she had a piece of string, old bakery string, around her hair, so that the mass of whiteness was off her face, and her eyes stood out more than ever. But she wore no shoes, and her dress was the same ragged mess of the day before. Clare did not want to stare at her, and so tried to look past, rather than at her.

"And how are your mother and father, Miss Clare?"

"Fine, thank you. And yourself, Mrs. Stevens?"

"Just fine."

This exchange of solicitude was spoken across the stench of Mrs. Stevens, so powerful it almost erased the salt breeze from the sea, only a hundred yards away.

"My, but you are a lovely girl. A beauty I think you may become."

"Thank you," Clare answered automatically, well taught that compliments about the way she looked were to be accepted in that way.

"But beauty is, of course, as beauty does, and you must mind what happens to you. So don't let them cross you up."

"Pardon?"

"Don't let them cross you up, that's all."

"No, Mrs. Stevens, I won't."

"Please call me Miss Winifred. I was never really Mrs. Stevens."

"Yes, ma'am."

"But they can cross you up so easily, you see. You may not even know you are being crossed up. Your mind may be on other things."

"Yes, Miss Winifred."

"Yes—yes, indeed—I know whereof I speak. I had a little girl once, you see. A long time ago. Over sixty years ago. But because her father was a coon and I had let a coon get too close to me . . . because I had a little coon baby, they took her away from me. The nuns took her and put her in one of their back-rooms where they put such children, and wouldn't let me see her at all. Her father was a coon, you see, but he was a nice man. I didn't even touch the little girl after she was born. I just saw her dark little head under the blanket the nuns wrapped her in. Her eyes were still shut tight, so I don't know what color they were—blue like mine, or black like her papa. They crossed me up but good, as you can easily see."

Clare had never heard a grown-up woman talk like this. She was embarrassed by the intimacy of Mrs. Stevens's words. Caught between politeness—not wanting to hurt Mrs. Stevens, not wanting to ask too much—and needing to know more about her. No grown-up had ever been so bare before her, and she was confused.

"What happened to your husband?"

"Heavens, my dear, he wasn't my husband. You can have babies without holy sanction, you know. Perhaps you don't know as yet."

Clare knew of course, but didn't know if she was supposed to know, since no grown-up had told her anything before this. And she didn't know what else to call the father of Miss Winifred's baby.

"Yes, ma'am."

"They wouldn't have let him be my husband in a million years. He was just a nice little Black man who worked for us. Who taught me how to grow things besides babies. To graft mango trees. To swim in the sea in front of the reef and to dive into the weeds at the bottom with a hollowed reed for the air to pass through. But when they asked me who the baby's father was, I said a ram-goat had run me down on a hillside and rutted with me.

"When my father found out who he was, he did away with him."

"I'm sorry."

"Yes. And they sent me to the convent. And that was that."

"I'm sorry."

"They punished him because I had a baby for him. They punished me because I let a coon get too close to me. But their punishment lacked imagination—they were just acting according to their tradition."

"What happened to your little girl?"

"I have no idea. I expect the nuns raised her up. Maybe she became a nun herself. She would be an old woman now. If she is still alive. Maybe she's dead."

Clare was waiting for the woman to stop talking and tell her she had made the whole story up. As she spoke, the eyes of Mrs. Stevens were bright. The center of the pupil was only a pinpoint of black in the broad sunshine. The iris was a purple flower flecked with yellow, and the white around the iris a cartography of red veins. Veins which broke in tiny explosions here and there. The eyes were still beautiful but the veins gave her life away. What she felt about that life. Up close the face was striking, elegant—a long aquiline nose almost meeting a full-lipped mouth. When she talked, her face moved. And when it moved, the dirt which masked her skin cracked, and fine lines were traced along her cheeks and beside the corners of her mouth and eyes. Her face seemed etched in an intricate pattern—so deep was the dirt and the lines across it. The eyes sparked in such a way that Clare knew the woman was relating something which was vivid to her, something she had not made peace with—not something she had invented in what Miss Beatrice called her madness.

"Your daughter . . . did you give her a name?"

"Only to myself. Only a name I call her to myself."

The woman stepped forward to touch Clare's face—and the girl drew back. "Makes no never mind," Miss Winifred muttered, dropping her hand and going on with her story.

"I think about her all the time. All the time. But what I did was wrong, you see. I knew better. I knew that God meant that coons and buckra people were not meant to mix their blood. It's not right. Only sadness comes from mixture. You must remember that."

"But, Miss Winifred, there's all kinds of mixture in Jamaica. Everybody mixes it seems to me. I am mixed too. My mother is red."

She admitted what she had been afraid to admit to Miss Beatrice. Maybe it was becoming time. Maybe she was relying on the confusion in Miss Winifred's mind. So she might take it back.

"Yes. Yes, they mix. And you are mixed. I know all that. And where has it gotten them? Where has it gotten you with your freckles? Don't you think I see the curls in your hair? They will become kinks the next thing you know. Your nose will broaden. And then where will you be? Just another coon-baby. That's all.

"All the water in the world cannot wash away what I did. My sad life. Which made another sad life. All the salt in the world cannot draw out the infection I carry in me. I live in repentance for my sins. I am not what I was meant to be."

"What do you think you were meant to be?"

"Not a filthy old lady, that's what I know. Not a woman afraid of water like most people are afraid of death. I was born to be somebody and I let that pass.

"I used to think that all of us on this island came from the sea when the sea spit us out. That we began our existences as fishes, and turned into people and birds and cattle and mongeese too. I used to think our island was a world born by chance, but that there was order and purpose after its birth.

"But of course that is not how it was. They brought people here in chains and then expected to prosper. They killed off all the Indians and all the snakes and believed they were doing good.

"Do you know about the ship called the *Zong*?" She paused only briefly, not waiting for an answer. "The *Zong* was a slave ship and the captain spilled the living bodies of Africans over the side, saying that they were infected. They were not infected. The captain collected insurance money for their souls. That is the sort of thing that went on here day after day.

"They are all gone now—the ones who did these things—gone to their reward. But the afterbirth is lodged in the woman's body and will not be expelled. All the waste of birth. Foul-smelling and past its use.

"You probably do not understand what I say to you."

The sound of the Packard turning the bend toward the house was heard by both of them.

"Come and talk to me again sometime." And she turned and was gone.

⌒

That night Clare dreamed that she and Zoe were fist-fighting by the river in St. Elizabeth. That she picked up a stone and hit Zoe underneath the eye and a trickle of blood ran down her friend's face and onto the rock where she sat. The blood formed into a pool where the rock folded over on itself. And she went over to Zoe and told her she was sorry—making a compress of moss drenched in water to soothe the cut. Then squeezing an aloe leaf to close the wound.

When she woke the power of the dream was still with her. But soon the dream was covered by her consciousness and a sharp pain in her vagina. It felt as if the lips were being pulled back and forth from within. Her pussy throbbed and hurt—the tops of her thighs felt heavy, filled up. She touched herself with her finger and found blood. Silently she got up, careful not to wake Miss Beatrice, and went into the back of the house and down the steps outside. Perhaps propelled by her dream, perhaps because she could not think of anywhere else to go, she headed for the stream formed by the cascades of water. She knelt beside the water and washed herself. It was icy cold, but the water numbed the cramps in her vagina and made her feel better. She folded a linen handkerchief into several layers and pinned it to her underpants. Her face was hot, and she dipped it in the water, catching her own likeness even though it was barely light.

Then she returned to the house and sat at a corner of the verandah. The sun was just rising in the direction of Ocho Rios. Her diary was in her lap, and she was writing about what she had woken to.

The numbing of the cold water was wearing off and Clare was slowly becoming accustomed to this new pain in her. The cramps in the lips of her pussy were now echoing off the walls of her inside. As the blood lining of her womb was breaking away.

When she got muscle cramps from exercise, Kitty told her it was a "sweet pain" and nothing to worry about. Something which would pass. Something which only meant that her body was working as it should—the tissues moving in reaction to exertion. Clare pictured the flesh of her insides expanding and contracting, then settling. This was not the same kind of pain, but it had its own sweetness, and promise that it would pass. All had happened as Zoe said it would. She shifted in her chair and felt a rush of warmth between her legs. She had another linen handkerchief in her grip should she need it.

The old lady came out to feed the birds. But she said nothing to Clare—who glanced at her, then turned back to her book. Something had happened to her—was happening to her. And it didn't really matter that there was not another living soul to tell it to.

She was not ready to understand her dream. She had no idea that everyone we dream about we are.

Glossary

battyman, homosexual male. equivalent of "faggot."

buckra, white person; specifically one representing the ruling class. British. (also *backra*.)

degga-degga, adjective used to emphasize a lack; e.g., I have not one degga-degga shilling.

donkey's years, a long time.

duppy, ghost; spirit.

e'en, even.

fe, for; of; to.

lignum vitae, tree of life.

mauger, skinny.

mek, allow; let. make.

ñam, eat.

pickney, child; children.

say, say; also, to know.

sheg-up, messed-up.

sint'ing, something. a word used broadly and with a variety of connotations.

smaddy, somebody. a word used as broadly as *sint'ing*.

teef, to steal; a thief.

wunna, you.

wuth, worth.

wuthless, worthless.

yerry, hear.

By Michelle Cliff

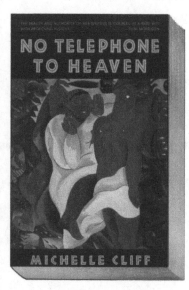

978-0-452-27569-0

978-0-452-27483-9

"**The beauty and authority of her writing is coupled in a rare way with profound insight.**"
—**Toni Morrison**

Plume
A member of Penguin Group (USA)
www.penguin.com

PO #: 0003275733